UNLOCKED

A collection of stories Edited and curated by

CHARLOTTE VALENTINE

Created with Vellum

Dedication

To those who have lost their lives to Covid-19 and to the family and friends who mourn their loss.

To those who continue to suffer from the effects of Covid-19.

To the brave healthcare professionals who have risked their lives to treat and support others. We can never thank you enough.

To the scientists who have persevered in their search to find a vaccine that can confront the virus and restore our lives to the 'normality' we all crave.

We dedicate this collection to you with love, respect and admiration.

Editor's Introduction

Welcome to *UNLOCKED*. I am thrilled to introduce you to this collection - thirteen unique stories, from thirteen unique women, written during the unique circumstances of the 2020 lockdown.

IN MARCH 2020, I launched a Lockdown Writing Challenge; open to aspiring, but unpublished writers. The task was to write a short story; the prize was the opportunity to be included in my short story collection, *LATE NIGHT SHOTS*, which was published in September 2020.

THE WINNER WAS Laura Cation whose story you are now about to read as the first in this collection. However, I was so delighted with the variety and originality of the other stories I received that I decided I wanted to publish as many of them as possible. It seemed a pity not to share the previously unlocked potential of these writers. And so *UNLOCKED* was born.

. . .

IT HAS BEEN my privilege to edit the stories you are now about to read. I have done so with a determination to retain the unique charm and personality of each story and its storyteller. It has been a pleasure to work with these writers - who have now become published authors - and to get to know them as individuals.

GIVEN the circumstances from which these stories emerged, all royalties from sales of *UNLOCKED* will be donated to the following charities:-

NHS CHARITIES TOGETHER - to support UK National Health Service staff and volunteers who are caring for those affected by coronavirus.

COVID-19 SOLIDARITY RESPONSE FUND - coordinated by the World Health Organisation (WHO), supporting countries to prevent, detect and respond to the pandemic.

ON BEHALF of all the authors who have contributed a story to *UNLOCKED*, and me, thank you for buying or downloading the collection and contributing to our chosen charities.

I HOPE you enjoy reading the stories.

Charlotte Valentine

1

YOU MUST STAY INSIDE

To mum and dad who always taught me to do my best at everything. I miss and love you both so much.

by Laura Cation

His head hurt. He thought he could hear a pounding siren somewhere. Was that really surprising for London?

Joel Connor opened his eyes slowly to find himself on the floor of what looked like a stock room, staring at the spine of "1984" by George Orwell. On the other side he was met with Aldous Huxley's "Brave New World". As a fanatic of classic books, he had read both eagerly by the time he was eight. Now, at ten years old, it was somehow reassuring to be reunited with them, especially in the confusion he found himself in.

Wait a minute. Now he remembered. His mum sounding panicked. Angry voices telling her she shouldn't be out. Her pushing him into this room out of sight. The virus. They were taking a chance being out, being seen - but she just wanted to spoil him, give him some escapism from this awful pandemic taking over the capital.

A mysterious virus had come from nowhere. Appeared in the form of orange smoke. An unusual smell. A virus that hit your immune system, infected your blood stream. If you refused to isolate yourself from society, away from others…death was the only option - or being put into compulsory isolation by the pandemic police.

They were everywhere in the city.

Getting up, he looked around. Absorbing his favourite smell. Old antiquarian books…seeing his favourite sight; shelves of books in dark, cosy alcoves in the "Absolutely Antiquarian and Coveted Collectible Bookshop".

Sitting curled up in a corner of his bedroom with a classic novel was all he wanted to do: a loner not interested in "Fortnite" or the latest craze on "Tik Tok". He thought about his mum. Where was she now? Try. Try to remember. Sadly, his mind was writing a blank page.

Joel looked out of the window feeling a wave of uneasiness. No one. Nothing, except…silence. He couldn't even work out whether the alarm he had heard before had stopped, or perhaps his mind was playing tricks. He felt the familiar sensation that had come over him so often before. Chest tightening. Dry mouth. Short…gasps…for…air.

'Keep calm, count to ten…it's fine, you just need to see what's happening. You're fine.' he kept saying to himself in his head.

He stepped outside the shop and looked along Marylebone High Street. No one in sight. His heart started pounding again as he put one foot in front of the other, heading away from the familiar - the comforting presence of books, to, what had appeared to be an eerie emptiness.

An area of London suddenly devoid of cars, buses…PEOPLE.

'Hello?' he called out. 'Hello?!'

A little louder now. Almost echoing. Again, all he was met with was silence. Walking along further, a flier blew down at his feet. Picking it up, he read three words emblazoned on it: "You are warned." He read on to the small print: "You are unsafe in London. There is a virus that will attack your immune system and result in rapid death. You must stay at home. Anyone found disobeying this instruction will face the wrath of the pandemic police."

Joel had heard his classmates talking about the virus at school but hadn't really paid any attention.

The teacher would sneeze. 'Hey watch Miss! You've got the virus! Don't give us it!' they sniggered.

Now he felt a rising panic at the dilemma of heading back to the shop to stay safe or keep going to find his mum. He decided. Keep going. He had to find her. Had to know for sure. A voice came from nowhere making him jump:

"Deaths caused by the virus now at 1,272…vaccine to be produced in July. Please remember if you are found outside you will be punished severely. We see everything."

As quick as it started, the message came to an end. Sounding like it had come through an old, crackly speaker.

JOEL FOUND HIMSELF OUTSIDE "MADAM TUSSAUDS" waxwork museum. The sign on the door said "Museum temporarily closed. Virus is spreading. Please stay at home."

It was bizarre to see no queue outside halfway round the block. Turning away he came face to face with two figures. He gasped seeing them dressed in white with hoods and visors attached and wearing white surgical gloves. Face to face with pandemic police on patrol.

'You are not supposed to be out!' one of them announced, slightly muffled. 'You will need to be punished!'

His mind went back to how it all began. This voice sounded like the one he heard in the book shop shouting at his mum.

Joel tried to make a run for it, but he had no hope with these two, barely identifiable figures grabbing an arm each. They put a blindfold over him and pulled him along.

'Help!' he cried. 'Someone?!'

They scoffed beside him. 'Do you seriously think anyone will hear you?! That there will be anyone out?! You should know this is why YOU must be punished!'

'But I…'

'Silence! We will hear no more of this!'

Joel felt the wave of panic again rise up from his stomach. As they pulled him blindly along, he had no idea where they were taking him. He was now indeed facing the wrath of the Pandemic Police. He felt himself flying and landing on what appeared to be a pile of rubbish bags.

'You will stay here now until we decide what we will do with you!'

THE DOOR SLAMMED SHUT and he whipped off his blindfold. Before he could think about his anxiety, he heard a voice emerge from a corner.

'Who's that? Is there someone there?'

The comforting voice he knew so well evaporated all the panic and confusion.

'Mum? Mum, is that you?!'

'Joel?? Oh Joel, I'm over here! Can you crawl over to me?'

Eagerly he crawled over to where he heard her voice, finding her looking pale but overjoyed to see him.

'Oh Joel! I am so pleased to see you! I hope you understand why I had to leave you there?'

'Yes. I do…but now they have found us both and I have no idea what will happen!'

They could hear a rustling sound across from where they were sitting, and a light appeared from nowhere shining on to a mouse that was crawling around. Then Joel saw a gap, big enough to crawl through. His mum turned to him.

'Joel! Do you see that gap? I'm sure it will be big enough for us to get through, what do you think?'

'Yes, I see it…and anything is worth a shot right now!'

He followed his mum over to the gap, crawling behind, looking at his hands from time to time, checking there were no more mice around. He wasn't keen on mice, but all that should matter now was getting out of here. Carefully they inched through the gap, feeling puddles underneath their fingers and a stench of raw sewage.

'Are you OK Joel?' she asked him every five minutes or so.

'Yeah, mum, I'm fine…just keep going!'

It felt like forever. Somewhere, in the distance, even more muffled now was the crackled speaker.

"Deaths caused by the virus now at 2,500…vaccine to be produced in September. Please remember if you are found outside you will be punished severely. We see everything."

It was almost on a loop, but with different information now on when a vaccine would become available…death rate rapidly increasing.

They continued their slow crawl; this was like a tunnel,

with twists and turns. He felt they would never reach the end of this long passage…but then a glimpse of light.

'Look Joel! We're nearly there!' his mum gasped.

'Yes!' he replied, but already wondering what was on the other side.

They moved forward faster now, shuffling along on their elbows.

'Here, Joel…we can get out now!'

His mum dropped down on her hands and edged her way towards the light until her legs finally went through last. Joel followed her with her easing him out. Looking around they saw they were on Baker Street. She took his hand.

'Come on! We have to make our way home from here without being seen!'

THEY HURRIED along a desolate Baker Street. A car with four blown tyres. A child's pram left. An abandoned brief-case. Glancing at him slowing down to look, Joel's mum stopped.

'Joel, we don't have time to look around now…we need to keep going, come on! You've been doing so well!'

Moving quickly again, they heard something behind them. Footsteps. Joel gasped.

'Mum! I can hear someone behind us!'

'Keep going, come on…we need to speed up! Let's run!'

He kept up with her. The Pandemic Police, no doubt. His chest tightened.

His mum gasped suddenly.

'Joel? Can you smell that?'

An unusual smell in the air, something he could not even describe. Nothing he had smelt before.

‘Yes! Mum, can you see that in front of us?’

Orange smoke. Twisting and turning as if caused by smoke from a fire.

‘Joel…I can’t breathe…’

‘Mum…I can’t either, what’s happening?’

They both sank to the ground. Gasping for air. Feeling their eyes smart. As they lay on the pavement two white figures appeared beside them.

‘We told you to stay indoors…’ they said, just as a crackly message came over the city again.

"DEATHS CAUSED by the virus now at 2,502...vaccine to be produced in December. Please remember if you are found outside you will be punished severely. We see everything."

2

THE WHITE HART

"Not all who wander are lost" (J.R.R. Tolkien 'The Riddle of Strider' from 'The Lord of the Rings')

by Amy Spaughton

September
Royal Forest
Scotland

In, out, in, out, in...

Breathe slow, breathe steady. Don't strike too soon, don't strike too late. Life had been reduced to its simplest units; cause and effect, action and reaction. Then why was he hesitating? His path had never been clearer.

Shoot, hit. Hit, find. Find...

That was it. He didn't know what the finding led to anymore. Resolution? Peace? *Don't be ridiculous. There was no peace.* He had been content to stare into the middle distance and ignore the finish line up until now. Part of him didn't believe he would make it this far. But the end had come. It had innocently trotted into his line of sight, its glistening downy chest puffed out in frightening certainty.

This was it. Shoot, hit, kill the white hart. Discover the truth. Find...

May
The Celtic Knot Haberdashery and Wool Shop
Edinburgh

HE SHUFFLED HIS FEET UNCOMFORTABLY. His broad figure stuck out from its cosy and colourful surroundings like a silhouette against a tropical sunset. Although he was surrounded by every shade and hue of every colour that could be imagined, he could only answer this cornucopia with dull browns that ranged from the worn leather of his tired coat to the greasy chestnut of his neglected hair. The bright wools and cheerful swathes of cloth seemed to shy away from him, as if his very existence in the same world was a personal affront to them. The shop's owner had much the same reaction to the stranger's presence when he bounded in from the back room. The two observed each other with confusion and unease for a moment before the owner nervously broke the silence.

'May I help you, sir?'

'I was told this is where I could find…'

'Ah, an American, may I ask where you originate from, sir?' the owner interrupted with a relaxed smile as if this explained everything.

'Colorado, I'm looking for a Mr…'

'Colorado, you say.' He mused on this happily. 'Interesting wildlife if I remember correctly. Lots of mountains and such like, reminds me of…'

'I'm looking for Mr Cernunnos.' he blurted out impatiently.

'Well, you have found him.' Mr Cernunnos replied sharply. 'What can I do for you?'

'I want you to tell me everything you know about the white hart.'

Mr Cernunnos' expression softened. 'I thought it a bit unlikely you were here for one of my knitting patterns.' He chuckled. 'I am always happy to talk history, particularly the myths and tall tales of my own country.' He beamed. 'What would you like to know?'

'I want to know how to find it.' he said directly.

Mr Cerunnos took the stranger in. His whole being screamed firm and undying fortitude, all stubborn fists and a resolute jaw. All, that is, but his eyes. His eyes tentatively whispered a torturous desperation.

The owner recoiled from him in hardened disgust, breathing deeply and silently while he considered his answer. 'I have seen enough men driven to madness looking for ghosts that ought to be left alone to know another one when I see it. Follow me.'

September
Royal Forest
Scotland

WHY WAS HE HESITATING? He was one motion away from his goal, away from the conclusion of a year-long quest.

Who was he fooling? It was an obsession, in its purest

form. And yet... One easy motion and it would be dead. Perhaps that was it. It was too easy. Months of mindless searching concluded by the movement of a single digit on a trigger. His glorious torture come to an end. *No!* He was overthinking things. Find it, kill it. That was all. But his logic had finally run dry. He was scratching at the brittle foundations he had hurriedly constructed for himself. They had been worn out by his journey and so had he.

He was a master of suppression. He had managed to reduce a burning, screaming maelstrom of fear, loathing and isolation into nothing more than an all- encompassing tint around the edges of his life. One that created a comfortable dizziness, as if the entire world had simply shifted slightly to one side. The most impressive part of this charade, however, was the central falsehood to which all of the veil was tethered. That at the moment of impact he had somehow been reborn into a quest-driven hero bent on discovery. He had separated his new reincarnation from his past life so expertly that he couldn't see past his own camouflage. He had peeked and caught tiny glances but that was all he could face. Until now.

Now it was unavoidable. He hadn't so much discovered it as it had discovered him. The truth stood brazen and unafraid before him. The marble grip that had dragged him, despairing, through the dirt and forgotten bones and blood to this point was no longer hidden.

Then surely the solution was simple. By shooting it, he would be free. He stared intensely at his inactive fingers on the trigger. At least that's what he told himself he was staring at. In reality he was staring at the gold band around his finger, his one indestructible tie to his past. The one tie that gripped him with an unwavering and conflicting strength that both forced him onwards and held his finger from the trigger.

April
The Joan Blackwood Library
Lyndhurst

MISS ROWE HAD BEEN OBSERVING a strange figure from her desk behind the thrillers section for the past hour. A crumpled statue sitting at a table in the centre of the room. Despite the ten or twenty books and articles laid out before him, he seemed to be appalled by every page. It was as if the texts were personally insulting him by bringing up unwarranted memories. When she had tried to nonchalantly look over his shoulder, although there was no need for her to be covert, she had found him transfixed by a picture of Richard II's emblem. The white hart sat up proudly, a golden crown acting as a leash around its neck.

The strange visitor stared at the trapped animal and the hart seemed to stare back at its mesmerised prisoner, snickering. He was a man waiting for the next crushing blow. The King of the land of in-between, he was a master of avoiding living. In a singular instant he had aged as if living through the eternal trudge of a silent journey. Reborn in a moment of helpless despair, he had started a tightrope walk towards a hazy future, stopping only to refuel in the bliss of his memories. Snapping out of his bliss only to find himself even further from the safety of the ground; a messy, wailing mix of anger and resolve propelling him forward, staggering dangerously.

His research had led him to the UK. He had stumbled from library to library, museum to museum, expert to expert, investigating any scrap of information that might lead him to the white hart. He had left in his wake a sea of confused and disgruntled people. He spoke only of three things - food, shelter and the white hart.

September
Royal Forest
Scotland

IN HIS HESITATION, he had been forced to loosen his grip. The facade that had nourished him and moulded him had fallen away. He lay, a free-standing figure without its supports. He was suddenly and irreversibly sentient.

There was a silence that he could not understand.

Expecting anger, fear and isolation - anything to animate him - he received only confusion and a dim sadness. Logically, if his suppression had ended then he should return to the state he was in at his trigger point.

Reluctantly, he recalled the day.

The memories returned to him tentatively. The feeling of safety as he trudged around the forest that he knew every inch of. The accomplishment of falling into his scruffy armchair after a long day. Gazing through the window at the view he had memorised like a pattern in the wallpaper. The initial memories were so mundane he wasn't sure they weren't false. They could have come from any day of his life in that house.

HE FELT her warmth against his cheek as she gave him a welcome home kiss. Her fingers had been taut, straining against her foe.

HE STARED INTENSELY at the creature now in his sights.

. . .

HE SMILED as her hair fanned out while she spun around and around. Her white linen dress had fallen at sharp angles around her. It was dirty and creased as usual but now too still.

THE WHITE HART bowed its head to sniff the wet ground.

He breathed deeply and tried to focus on specific aspects of the creature. Its marble fur. Its glassy eyes. Its shifting hooves.

HE HAD ALWAYS WATCHED her fingers. Long and elegantly curved, she would act out her words with them like a secret second language.

But then her body had been completely inactive; only her eyes and mouth had moved. Her eyes pleaded with him and her lips quivered. She muttered incomprehensibly while he begged her to stop, to save her strength. With a sudden jolt of pain, she gained enough adrenaline to grab his collar, pulling her tensed body up slightly from where he cradled her head.

'You will find it, the white hart, you must promise me…' She rasped, frightened by some unknown danger.

'Help is coming…' he begged.

'No.' she interrupted. 'You must promise.'

'Anything, I promise.'

THE WHITE HART turned its head slowly towards him as if it had known he was there all along. He wondered if it knew its own significance. He admitted it didn't look the way she had drawn it. He could remember the animation in her voice when she told him of her day's findings. The content was hidden under another level of suppression.

He tightened his grip on the trigger. Breathe in, breathe out and just do it. Finish it. End the creature. He had promised. If he didn't then his last words to her were lies.

Unexpectedly and all at once, the veil lifted. All of his memories escaped his suppression and were clear. Her obsession; to his obsession; to now. She was ill and mad and fixated on the white hart. She had researched as he had; as uninterested in anything other than her goal as he was.

She had drawn grotesque drawings of her imagined future victory over the beast and plastered them around the house like motivational posters. He was happy she was alive, so he had ignored her obsession. He had minimised her madness to a hobby. But her hobby had seeped into the groundwater, lying dormant until the dam had burst. Her death had broken the seal on those memories, forcing him to re-enact her obsession like a perverse rerun.

If her death had started this, then surely the death of the white hart would finish it. In a perfect world the symmetry would complete the cycle. But he was imperfect, he had been warped by his journey. At this thought, he abandoned his logic, his instincts, and his weapon and staggered to his feet.

The white hart observed him in silent stillness. He took a tentative step forward, his hand outstretched in supplication.

The white hart bolted without looking back.

3

INHERITED

For Rob, who has always encouraged, supported, and humoured me. For my parents, who have always fed my love of reading and gave me the freedom to be me. All my love.

by Penny Coke - Woods

ANSA WATCHED the plane take off with a tightening chest. From the jetty she could see her mother looking back at her through the passenger porthole. It had been an unexpectedly tearful goodbye. For her whole life the two of them had had each other, whatever happened Ansa knew her mother would be there. She was her safety line. They relied on each other for everything and now, for the first time in her twenty-four years, Ansa would be without her. As the plane left the surface of the water and climbed further away Ansa could feel the safety line stretch, pulling the knot in her chest tighter. Her breath quickened as the plane gained altitude. It was too far away to see her mother now. The last impression she had was of a pale face framed in the oval window. Still, she looked after the plane hoping to stay connected for just a bit longer. A hand slipped into hers and she started.

'Ready to go in?'

Ansa sighed and nodded. The fog from her breath merged with the mists that rose from the pine forest and drifted across the lake. The surface of the water calmed quickly from the ripples caused by the seaplane's take off. Soon it would be as if it had never been there. Breaking her gaze away from the vanishing plane, she looked up at her new husband. She'd always had someone to rely on, someone to tie her safety rope to. Up until now that line had run to her mother. Now it was cut and newly attached to her husband.

Snaking his arm around her, Jaakob led Ansa down the jetty and towards her new home. She didn't turn to see the plane swallowed by the heavy clouds.

THIS WAS the first time Ansa had been to her husband's estate. She had known he was wealthy. His family had owned swathes of land all over Finland for centuries, but all she had known of it was the fashionably minimalist apartment he owned in Helsinki. Despite being from an old money family, Jaakob Partanen had played the modern urbanite well. He had not embarrassed himself with over extravagance but neither had he been needlessly frugal.

They had met at a party neither of them wanted to be at. Both had gone to support friends; she to talk her friend up to a prospective employer, he to introduce his friend to a woman. With both their tasks accomplished they had found each other lingering by the food table contemplating the pros and cons of the canapés. Conversation between them was easy and before the night was over, she'd fallen for him completely. To begin with Ansa knew him only as Jaakob, his family name held no special significance to her. Their romance was not grand or showy, rather it was intimate and comfortable. More often than not they could be found folded around each other on Jaakob's sofa, snacking on junk food and watching nothing in particular on TV. It wasn't until the second month of their romance, however, that she realised just how wealthy he was and what that meant.

Jaakob had taken them to a chic new eatery to celebrate Ansa's birthday. It was the only thing she'd asked for and she hadn't questioned that he'd booked the table under her name. Her stomach fluttered when they arrived, the restaurant was entirely out of Ansa's usual sphere of experience. Her new dress made her look the part of a refined socialite, but in every other way she felt completely unprepared for it. There had been some disagreement when Jaakob talked to the host. Apparently, there was no booking under Ansa's name and despite Jaakob's insistence on the matter the maître'd had smiled a sickly, placating smile and likewise insisted that they were full. Jaakob had looked conflicted but after seeing Ansa's crestfallen look he turned back to the host and, leaning close to him, had whispered something. The host's jaw had dropped in shock and he'd almost fallen over himself to loudly make his apologies to 'Herra Partanen'.

In moments a table became available and they were informed that complimentary champagne would be waiting for them when they were seated. Jaakob had accepted the gifts with a tight smile. As they passed through the restaurant Ansa became aware of excitable mutterings from the other diners. Throughout their meal she noticed the consistent and poorly hidden glances from the patrons. They were the centre of attention and it was making her as uncomfortable as Jaakob looked. Ansa downed her free champagne and tried to ignore the incessant chattering around them. Jaakob didn't touch his glass, he sat on his hands looking tense. They tried to hold their own conversation while knowing they were the subject of all the other ones going on around them. Eventually they gave up and pushed their food around in silence. Ansa had been so excited to go out, but if every time they were out together they were going to be faced with this same experience she wasn't sure she could handle it. The only thing she knew for certain was she loved Jaakob more than anything.

She leaned across the table and spoke quietly, 'Can we get out of here?'

Jaakob looked at her unsure, 'Are you sure? It's your night.'

'This isn't what I want. I just want to be with you.'

Jaakob beamed and they were gone before dessert.

Later that week he asked her to move in with him. Ansa asked him then about the restaurant, why he didn't use his family name when it would open all kinds of doors for him. He'd said that he didn't feel like he had the right to use it. His parents had both died when he was a child and he hadn't known them. He didn't feel in the least connected to his family name. He'd said that his money gave him enough of an advantage, he just wanted to live quietly with the woman he loved. He attributed his lack of ambition to being raised by a guardian. Losing his parent's so young, he said, taught him how painful life could be and that being rich did not protect him from the cruelty of the world.

He did not like to talk about his family. There were a few times Ansa had gotten him to talk about his mother but every time she pressed on the subject of his father a dark cloud passed over Jaakob that could not be lifted without effort. No amount of coaxing or distraction could pull him back to himself, it was something that seemed to follow him around and Ansa had learned over time to avoid the subject altogether. As a result, she knew very little about his parents and even less about the Partanen family. The only thing that she had managed to learn was that his father was dead and that Jaakob did not miss him.

The Partanen family estate was ostensibly huge but from her vantage point on the jetty Ansa could only see snow, pine trees and the peaks of far off mountains. It would take forty minutes of patient tramping in snow shoes to reach the edge of the formal gardens and a further fifteen to reach the front door. It was going to be a tough trek to the house but with Jaakob by her side she felt invulnerable. Each step she took she fell in love with the landscape a little bit more. The thick snow smothered all sound except for the crunch of their snow shoes. The dark, looming pines flanked them as they trudged onwards.

Eventually they broke through the tree line. Ahead of them the ground sloped gently downwards towards the estate. There were odd shapes poking out of the snow, jagged grey teeth breaking through the white; the remains of the wall marking the edges of the Partanen residence. It looked like the old stones had fallen down decades ago and no-one had seen the worth in building them up again. This far away from everything, Ansa reasoned, there wasn't much to keep out. Despite the dilapidated nature of it, she was glad to have finally reached the edge of the grounds. The sun was already setting and before long it would be unwise to go outside at all. Soon the outside world would no longer matter, she would be with Jaakob ensconced inside.

Past the ruined walls the path levelled out and Ansa could see lumps and bumps where rose bushes and plants hid under snowy caps. Come spring this garden would be filled with colour and perfume, but for now it was dormant.

As they crunched down the driveway the clouds broke a little. Ansa lifted her eyes to see her new home for the first time. The fractured sunlight caught the edges of several roof peaks each crowned with an ornamental metal spike. The front facade of the building was made of grey slate, stark against the colourless fog and snow. Its face was slotted with three dozen windows spanning two floors of ancient gothic splendour. They reflected nothing.

Ansa's step faltered. Once more she felt so ignorant of her husband's world. She never thought anyone actually lived in places like this but yet again she had underestimated the scale of her husband's wealth and the ancestry shadowing him. She was staggered by the scale of the property. She looked over her new home with the growing sense that the dark compound eyes of the house were staring back at her. All of a sudden, she realised how cold she was, and she shivered. Jaakob pulled her in close and planted a kiss on the top of her hood.

He tilted his head to the side to see her better, 'You okay?'

Ansa smiled up at him, feeling warm again as she found his shining grey eyes. 'Yes. I can't believe you live here.'

'*We* live here,' he corrected gently.

Her smile broke open into a grin, 'We.'

He reflected her grin, 'Come on, we'll warm up inside.'

THE THICK FRONT door creaked laboriously as it opened. As the light bulbs warmed up the odd shapes in the hall became defined objects. The house had inhabited generations of the Partanen family, each adding their own fingerprints to the decor. The inside of the building looked like it straddled time, 18th century salon chairs stood next to canvases of 1960's pop-art. Ansa found herself standing in a room of anachronisms, the modern next to the classical. The effect was disorienting.

Ansa glanced up at Jaakob. There was a peculiar strained look on his face that vanished as soon as he noticed she was looking at him. He took Ansa's hand and led her through the first of several doors that pocked the hallway. This one revealed a large modern-looking room dominated by a fire place and a large leather sofa draped in reindeer furs. He sat his new wife down on the soft leather and wrapped her up in the largest of the furs. He lit a fire and joined Ansa under the reindeer skin. They sat close, rubbing each other's hands to warm up. Jaakob moved his hands up his wife's arms, running them around her shoulders, pulling her into him. They stayed like this for a blissful while, listening to the fire.

'Shall I show you around?'

Ansa slowly shook her head, she had other ideas. Leaning into him she landed a long, slow kiss on Jaakob's lips.

Outside the snow began to fall.

Sometime later Ansa awoke. She lay in the glow of her memories for a moment before she realised something had changed. She reached out along the thick rug searching for her husband but found nothing. Lifting her heavy head from the floor she blinked sleepily as she scanned around her. Jaakob wasn't in the room. Groggily she got to her feet and padded out into the house. Outside the snow looked dirty in the pre-dawn light.

The entrance hall stretched away into the gloom. Methodically, she investigated the other rooms branching off the hall. Her search revealed a sitting room lined with pristine books, some of which still had their pages sealed; a neglected dining room with cabinets full of dusty silver; a pantry lined with tins and jars from which she selected a few biscuits as a travel snack; and a small musty room which seemed to exist purely to drink cognac in.

Still no Jaakob.

She followed the corridor round visiting each room in turn until she reached the dead end. There was no sign of her husband. Perhaps he was upstairs. She turned to make her way to the staircase when she felt a breeze brushing her bare ankle. A breeze that seemed to come from nowhere. There were no open windows or doors ajar that she could see and yet it was getting in from somewhere. Tracing back with her hand, she reached for the icy air until her finger tips brushed the seam of the wall at the corridor's end. Feeling with her fingers she followed the sliver of space around all four sides of the dead-end wall. There was a gap.

She caught something on the edge of her hearing. Operating on instinct she jumped back, and the end wall swung away from her. Jaakob emerged from the doorway. His brow was heavy set and his shoulders rounded with fatigue. He trod softly in padded socks, seemingly engrossed in his thoughts. When he looked at her, she saw his body tense and his eyes were ablaze. The force with which he slammed the door behind him rattled the pictures that hung around them. When he reached for her, Ansa jumped back, all at once terrified of a man she'd only ever known as gentle. Her movement broke his fury. The Jaakob she knew seemed to return.

'Ansa, my love, I'm so, so sorry. Forgive me, forgive me.' he begged.

Ansa felt a stone fist gripping her airway. She had never been so scared and like a sudden cold snap she realised all at once that there was no-one else in the house. There was no-one else nearby to help her. She was alone in a house she did not know, with a man she now realised was capable of a frightening fury.

'I don't understand.'

'I'm so sorry, Ansa. You startled me,' he said weakly.

'What's in there?'

Jaakob's jaw clenched, 'It's my father's study.'

'It's ours now, surely.'

'Not that place. It still reeks of him. Please, my dearest, this house is old and is full of memories and ghosts. I don't want you to have to carry the burden of my family. Can you please let me have this part as my own? You can find your own place and I won't intrude on it, but everything past this door must be for me only. Do not go down there.'

Ansa didn't understand. Jaakob had never before shown any desire to connect with his father and now he wanted to preserve this part of him. Jaakob saw nothing but doubt in Ansa's eyes.

'I would never hurt you.'

Ansa wanted so badly to believe him. Her safety line was fraying, and she wasn't sure she could live in a place like this untethered, adrift. Survival was to be found in reconciliation. She reached out her hand and he took it carefully despite his desperation for forgiveness.

'I love you, my darling wife. Come on, I'll make us some breakfast.'

IT WASN'T the fanciest breakfast but to Ansa it was the best meal she'd ever had. Everything tastes so much better when eaten in the presence of someone you love. As the kitchen began to glow with the dawn light Ansa began to appreciate the feeling of a love grown stronger after conflict. It hadn't taken much for Jaakob to reassure Ansa, she had wanted things to return to normal just as much as he did. Jaakob talked softly as he offered her apologies in the form of food. Ansa tried to lighten the atmosphere by making Jaakob laugh, showing him that everything was okay. With both of them working to clear the air they were soon giggling together, all sign of tension pushed away.

'What shall we do today?' she asked with a suggestive tone. Her boldness had returned with the warmth growing in her heart.

A small smile flickered momentarily across Jaakob's face, but he did not look at her. Instead he stared out at the fresh snow that had settled over night, and an encroaching heavy cloud that promised more.

'I have some things I need to finish. Why don't you explore the house?

Find yourself a room just for you?'

Ansa tried not to look disappointed, 'Maybe. I might try to take a walk around the gardens, at least while the sun is still shining.'

'Of course. I'll make sure I'm done by lunch and we can spend the rest of the day together. Doing whatever you want.'

'Whatever I want?' she raised an eyebrow.

'I promise.'

. . .

BY THE TIME Ansa had wrapped herself up in several fleece pullovers, thick trousers, layers of socks and finally strapped on her snow shoes the approaching cloud had settled over the house. As she pulled the front door open the wind blew snow into the hallway and sliced her cheeks with its frigid fingers. Outside it had whipped the snow up into a whitewash. There was no sky, there was no ground. There was nothing beyond the confines of the house. She wasn't going anywhere.

Putting all of her weight to the door she shut it against the wind. The brief exposure had left her thoroughly cold. Attempting to find some heat she stomped her way into the lounge with the glowing fireplace and added the reindeer furs to her layers. She found a remote control and with it a large TV hidden behind a mahogany panel. This is what she needed; an everyday comfort in the strange world of manors and secrets. After some tentative prodding the fire came to life from the few embers left from overnight. She sat heavily into the sofa and flicked through the channels, finally landing on an old episode of a crime drama she'd seen too many times. She sank further into the furs and fleece, not bothering to stifle her yawning. She was cozy now and unexpectedly tired. The morning had been a surprisingly full one and in retrospect she realised she hadn't got much sleep during the night. The soft glow of the fire and the gentle jabbering from the TV, lulled her into a comfortable sleep.

An hour later she woke with a start. Getting up before dawn, even a Finnish winter dawn, had made the mid-morning nap welcome. The room swam into focus and she sat up and enjoyed a long, slow stretch. There was a voice chattering somewhere nearby and it took Ansa slightly too long to realise it was coming from the TV. It had moved on to a grizzly true-crime documentary about a spate of disappearances thirty years ago. As Ansa shook off her sleepiness something caught her attention. The victims were all women, each in their mid-twenties, and each had gone missing shortly after getting married. The programme scrolled through images of them. It lingered on the last one; a photo of a joyful woman with dark hair and deep eyes that crinkled with her smile.

According to the reports, the men they had married had shared similar physical traits, in particular piercing grey eyes. The host theorised that the husbands were in fact the same person making the perpetrator a serial abductor. It was thought that each woman's last known whereabouts was a secluded area in the north of Finland. As the programme flashed up images of the area, something began to itch in Ansa's mind. There was something familiar about the landscape, the pine trees, the mountains in the distance, and the lake with a jetty nestled in amongst them. She tensed at that image; she was staring at their jetty on the water, less than an hour's walk from the house. The same jetty she had arrived at yesterday.

'Where could these women have been taken?' asked the programme, *'The jetty is used by several seasonal agricultural workers but also provides access to the secluded Partanen family home, ancestral house of one of Finland's wealthiest and oldest families.'*

Ansa's breath caught in her throat. Her mind came to a conclusion that she did not want to acknowledge. She stood still, suddenly certain she had to move, but not knowing in which direction. Jaakob had said this house was full of ghosts but surely this wasn't what he'd meant. She was just being spooked by stories. Maybe this is what he had wanted to shield her from; rumours and conspiracies, gossip and baseless accusations. She told herself it was all nonsense but still she couldn't stop herself moving onwards, away from the television and deeper into the house.

She came to the dead end of the corridor to find the hidden door slightly ajar. Upstairs she could hear the sound of water running. Jaakob wasn't in his father's study. She tried to convince herself that there was nothing to worry about. She told herself that if she went inside she'd find it all rather mundane. She tried to believe it, but nothing could smother the spark of doubt deep down. With trepidation Ansa pushed the door open. Ahead of her, a short passage led to a dim glow at the end, a desk lamp pushing away the shadows. Ansa made her way towards it with small shaking steps.

The passageway opened up into a narrow room dominated by an old, scratched writing desk, its surface piled high with papers. There were yellowing letters, old newspaper articles, and folders containing what looked like official reports. She struggled to make out the writing in the dim light of the room. Fear grew in Ansa as she saw some of the reports were emblazoned with the emblem of the *Poliisi*. She backed away from the mountains of evidence before her and lifted her gaze to the wall behind the desk. Ice filled her veins. Up on the wall, flanked by five others, was a photograph of the woman from the documentary, smiling with dark hair and deep eyes. The missing woman. One of the women who was last seen not five miles from this house.

Ansa's world spiralled into chaos. The foundations of the life she'd built for herself were shattered. Everything was thrown into question. How well did she really know Jaakob? How could she have agreed to come out to this isolated place? She was totally alone. All those decisions she'd been sure of before, were revealed for what they truly were; romantic naivety.

Ansa turned to escape the eyes, to flee the study. But as she tried to go, she saw the shelf next to the study's door and she froze. On the shelf stood six identical metal pots, each labelled with a name, a date, and an age.

She stood, petrified. It was true. It was all true. She knew it but she couldn't acknowledge it. Her breath stopped as her heart raced. She was adrift, lost, any connection to a place of safety severed. Her mind screamed at her to move as her body refused to do anything. A bead of sweat ran down her forehead and dropped to the floor. The small sound of it hitting concrete jolted her out of her daze. She flung off the furs and made to run out of the house, all regard for silence and secrecy forgotten.

In her fear she threw the front door open, once more allowing the blizzard winds to assault the hallway. Without hesitation she ran into the storm. Each step took enormous effort. The snow swallowed her up to the thigh. She carved through the drifts, her bare hands turning red then white then grey with the cold. The wind stole her breath. She could feel nothing but the burn in her throat and the sting of terror squeezing her heart. Her pace slowed even as she urged herself onwards. Her legs were leaden. She was frozen to her core and her vision was darkening. She faltered and fell deep into the snow. The wind screamed overhead, blowing snow onto her prone body. Every breath burned. As she slid into unconsciousness Ansa caught the sound of snow crunching and a voice on the air.

Something snapped on the edge of her hearing. Then silence. But then another snap, this time with crackling underlying it. Ansa's mind reeled as she realised she was awake and with it came the rush of new sensory information. Slowly she opened her eyes to see a fire roaring. Her neck ached as she tried to roll onto her back, but she only managed to tangle herself further in the many blankets wrapped around her. She tried to sit up, but her hands and feet were useless, somehow numb and throbbing agony at the same time. As she groaned something moved on the edge of her vision and she froze.

Jaakob was sitting by the fire with his head in his hands but when he heard Ansa awaken, he stood swiftly and moved towards her. Ansa recoiled as far as she could into the sofa. Jaakob faltered and stopped.

For a long while neither spoke. Outside the winds died away.

Eventually Jaakob found his voice.

'I'm so sorry, Ansa. You ran so fast I couldn't stop you. You'll be okay, you're not frostbitten. Why did you do that?'

Ansa remained still, cornered, and said nothing.

Jaakob's voice penetrated the silence.

'I hate this house. I would sell it, or burn it to the ground, but there is work I have to do before I can let it go.'

'Those women. You couldn't have… So, who…?'

'My father. He was monstrous, and rich enough to get away with it. My mother was fortunate; she got pregnant before he tired of her.'

'Why? Why keep it all? Take it to the police.'

'I know…'

'How? How could you keep this?'

'I know…'

'I can't live here. I can't stay here, I'm so scared.'

'I know,' he whispered.

'No, you don't. You don't understand. I can't stay in the house where those women died.'

Jaakob hung his head.

'Jaakob, please. Take it to the police. Be done with it. Be done with this place.' Ansa pleaded.

'I know I should but then I'll never be rid of it. Someone will find out. Someone will tell the world and then all I will be is the son of a monster. I can deal with it quietly. I can track down their families, return them home, make reparations. Then I can move on.'

Ansa tried to understand. She tried to see it from Jaakob's side, but it was all too much. Everything whirled and nothing made any sense. A single thought solidified in the storm.

'What about me?'

Jaakob grew afraid. He knelt by Ansa's side, his voice cracking as he spoke.

'I promised I would never hurt you. I will never hurt you. I am not my father.'

More than anything, Ansa wanted desperately to believe him. This time, however, survival couldn't to be found in reconciliation. Too much had occurred for her to push away. She'd have to find it somewhere else. There was no-one else and nothing else to do. For the first time her safety line anchored to something within.

'I believe you Jaakob. But I cannot live here. I'm leaving tonight for Helsinki. I love you. Come with me and love me there. Live your life, not the one your father left you.'

That evening a seaplane took off from the lake. Ansa didn't look out of the porthole choosing instead to focus on the view through the fight deck window. She explored the new feeling inside her, a feeling of stability, a feeling that she could rely upon herself before others. She smiled to herself, finally able to breathe amongst the clouds. A hand slipped into hers. She turned and looked into Jaakob's grey eyes. There was something new about him also; a lightness that suited him. He smiled too.

'Thank you. I love you.'

Ansa squeezed her husband's hand reassuringly, 'Me too.'

4

TO LEARN WHAT BELONGING WAS

A retelling of '*To Learn What Fear Was*' from The Brothers Grimm book of Fairy Tales

To all the cruise ship crew members who kept each other safe at sea this year.

by Alice Stansfield

There was once a girl who wanted a sense of belonging. She wanted to know her purpose in life and she wanted to succeed in finding happiness in where she belonged. This wasn't to say she wasn't happy; she just wanted to know she was in the right place, where she was meant to be. Her mother, her father, her brother and her friends had all said at some point in their life "this is where I belong" and sighed with relief. But the girl didn't know where "this" was. She didn't know where she belonged and, perhaps more importantly, she certainly didn't know how to get there.

'How do I know where I belong?' asked the girl of her mother.

'You'll just know.' replied the mother, seemingly without even a second thought.

'Do I know now?' she queried back.

'You tell me.'

The girl had no answer and felt even more lost than at the start of the conversation. She turned to her father.

'Father, where do you belong and how do you know?' the girl quizzed.

'I belong at home dear. I know that because I feel at home when I am home.'

'So that means I belong at home too because this is my home!' The girl smiled broadly.

The father raised his eyebrow. 'You belong where you feel you belong. Do you feel you belong at home?'

'I feel…I don't know.' She paused. 'I feel lost'.

She turned to her brother who had always seemed one step ahead of her in life, not just in age.

'Brother, how did you discover where you belonged?'

'I belong at work, because I enjoy it and I'm good at it. I discovered that by going out and working.'

'Then that is what I must do!' exclaimed the girl. 'I'll go out and work, and then I'll belong!'

After speaking with her mother, father and brother, the girl decided she could only know the place where she belonged by going out and finding it - whether that was through working, getting less lost, or looking anywhere but here. Her sense of belonging was out there somewhere.

And if nobody else could tell her where it was, then she was going to find it herself!

. . .

THE NEXT MORNING, she packed her satchel and took all her coins from the jar on her bedroom windowsill for her travels. She looked through her window at the mountain which overlooked her town. It was the tallest mountain she had ever seen in her entire life, and, in an instant, she decided that was where her sense of belonging might be. At least it would be a good starting place to begin her search. She said goodbye to her mother, her father and brother and vowed to get as un-lost as possible in order to find her sense of belonging. She needed to get to the top of that mountain. For hours she walked, climbed and crawled her way up to the peak of it and collapsed, exhausted, in the snow at the top. Shivering in its damp, wet iciness, she rolled to her side to be met with the magnificent view of the valley below. If she squinted carefully, she could see the faint detail of her house, as if it was sketched into the hillside.

She stared at her home, then back at the mountain, and wondered; did she feel a sense of belonging?

She asked the mountain. 'Is this where I belong?' The mountain didn't reply. Instead the silence was broken only by the whistle of the wind and the view from the top of the mountain grew dimmer as the light began to fade. Unsatisfied with the lack of an answer, she decided to head back down the other side of the mountain.

She sighed. Her journey to find where she belonged had not started well.

On her way down she found a trickling stream which danced and weaved between her steps. She followed it until it brought her to the edge of the largest waterfall she'd ever seen. The pool at the bottom of the waterfall shone rainbow reflections all around her, creating a hypnotising ocean.

She smiled. Her sense of belonging must be wrapped in the water. She couldn't resist diving in.

She looked up from under the water at the twinkling light bouncing on each tiny ripple towards the wave-filled sky. But she frowned; her sense of belonging wasn't there either. She felt exactly the same as she always did at home, except that she was submerged in water.

She began to wonder whether a sense of belonging was further away from home than she'd ever imagined.

FOR YEARS she travelled to many of the thousands of islands that surrounded her home to search for her sense of belonging. So many that she lost count.

She climbed more mountain peaks and at each summit, exhausted, she asked the clouds if this was where she belonged, but she received no answer.

She swam to the depths of the ocean to ask the murky darkness if this was where she belonged, but still no answer.

She followed rivers as far as they could take her but found no answers there.

She met villagers in far-away worlds that didn't even speak her language. She studied them and lived with them to see what their sense of belonging was, but she was merely a visitor, just passing through. So, her sense of belonging wasn't there either.

Tirelessly, she trekked through forests looking under every leaf and found nothing.

In the hot desert she knelt to her knees and whispered to the sand, asking its guidance to her sense of belonging, but the sand only blew away.

She met exotic animals in the jungle, dolphins in the water, trailed through botanic gardens, climbed the highest trees, and crawled through caves that threatened to suffocate her.

But still the world couldn't tell her where she belonged.

If nature couldn't tell her she would continue to find as many people as possible and ask them where she could find her sense of belonging.

She journeyed deep into the largest cities in the world. She was directed several times to 'Lost and Found' departments, only to discover her sense of belonging wasn't an object in a box.

In one particular town she found strangers who claimed their sense of belonging was there. They welcomed her, so she stayed a while. But she found no sense of herself there, so she moved on.

AFTER YEARS of searching for her own sense of belonging she reluctantly concluded she couldn't find one at all and admitted to herself that she had exhausted all of her options. With a heart full of a strangely heavy emptiness, she headed towards home.

She travelled back through villages, towns, cities and islands; deserts, jungles, forests and rivers; oceans, valleys, caves and gardens; waterfalls and mountains. As she passed through, she waved to all the wonderful people she had met on her journey. They came from different cultures, backgrounds and spoke many different languages. She recalled moments of peace with them all as they discussed their world and their sense of belonging within it.

She pictured herself back in each location; lying on top of the mountain, kneeling in the sand, swimming deep in the water - and she loved the feeling that filled her body with every memory. It made her journey home exciting, as she recalled each moment, minute by minute. Her journey had taken longer than she had ever thought possible, but it slowly began to feel like less of a failure after all.

As feelings of warmth pervaded her, she found herself back at the front door she'd walked out of so long ago.

Her mother, her father, and her brother all welcomed her return. They beckoned her in and sat her down. They asked her about all the adventures she'd had while they had spent years at home wondering if she had found her sense of belonging.

The girl took a deep breath and started from the beginning of her journey, telling them everything from the moment she had left the house and begun by pursuing the great mountain by their house. Although they lived so near it, none of them had ever thought to explore it; it had simply always been there. Even though the mountain was so near her father's home, which was where he felt he belonged, he admitted he'd barely given it a second glance in all his years. As the girl talked and moved on from the mountain to tell of the waterfall, lakes and oceans, the father peered out of the window at the mountain in the distance and tilted his head to one side.

The girl began to realise that on her return something had changed. As she shared the stories of her journey with her family, and then with her friends, no longer did she feel lost.

She felt as tall as the mountains she had climbed, her soul as deep as the oceans she had swum, her spirit as wild as the animals as she had met. She felt as beautiful as the flowers in the gardens she had seen, and yet as lost as everyone else in the world.

But she felt incomplete in a beautiful way because she realised she hadn't seen or done everything yet. She was merely on the edge of the map. She was only just beginning.

She belonged to the world and she owed it to the Earth to marvel in its gloriousness and explore its every grain.

From now on she would treasure and preserve the world. She would leave only footprints and take only memories.

Now - finally – she had her sense of belonging.

She belonged, because she lived.

And she would spend every day making the most of her life and her world.

5

VISION OF LOVE

To everyone affected by Covid-19. Especially those mourning the loss of their loved ones.

by Alison Apasa

Ellie was only fourteen when she lost her mother, and it devastated her.

She spent months trying to adjust to her new life as her heart was in pieces. With only her father to turn to, he became her lifeline.

They lived in a large house set back from the street. Unusually, the well- equipped kitchen was in the cellar, with a stone floor, blue walls and white cupboards over-looking the island worktop in the centre of the room. Ellie's mother had loved the many hours she spent there cooking and baking Ellie's favourite foods. The rest of the house had an old-fashioned, traditional feel to it.

The lounge was dominated by a large ornate coal fire-place with Victorian candle holders over the mantelpiece; they were black with tall white candles sitting within them.

The mirror above sat in an intricately patterned black metal frame. The grey corner sofa was filled with an array of large scatter cushions in blue, yellow and black, which Ellie tried to keep scattered in just the way her mother had.

To the left of the living room was a twisting staircase; bare wood stairs in white with a black handrail, leading to bedrooms filled with ornate beds with black metal head and foot rests.

Ellie loved her home; it was comfortable and cosy, and her mother's touch was everywhere.

She led an ordinary life; she spent a lot of time brushing her long curly locks of blonde hair and always remembered how her mother had loved it. 'Just like a princess.' she used to say. Ellie grew close to her father, James, a stout friendly man, popular with everybody and known to his friends as "Jim" or "Jimmy". After his wife died, he prioritised Ellie's needs above everything - working from home as much as possible and keeping the weekends free for them to spend time together grabbing a burger in town, playing monopoly or sharing popcorn over a movie.

And to simply sit and grieve together as they looked at old photos of happier times with her mother.

Ellie was almost sixteen the day her friend told her about the fancy-dress ball the entire village were excited about, the minute she walked through the school door.

'Ellie, wait there.' Rose shouted from the school corridor.

'Oh, Rose, it's you, hiya'.

'I'm so excited Ellie, have you seen the posters for the fancy-dress ball at the village hall? We have to go. Everybody's going to be there. And not just locals either I don't think. New people too.'

She laughed at Rose. Her friend was always happy and

today her excitement was infectious. 'It sounds great. When is it?'

'In six months, so it'll be our end of summer term celebration. You've got to go Ellie; and everyone who's anyone is going'. Rose paused to straighten her loose-fitting school uniform pink blouse and looked in her make up mirror as she checked her appearance. She smoothed her jet-black hair, which was tidy, short and plain but complemented her slim figure. She was trying to look sophisticated and it made Ellie smile.

'What would I wear; did you say it's fancy-dress?' asked Ellie, frowning in thought as she placed her bag into her locker.

'Yeah, why don't you go as a princess, that would suit you. And we all have to wear masks, so no one knows who anybody is. Such fun, I can't wait, I'm going to go as Queen Mary.'

'What? Ha! Ha!'

'Yeah, you can laugh'. They chattered away in the busy crowded corridor on their way to class. Ellie felt Rose's excitement about the ball, but as she sat in her drama lesson hearing other kids excitedly talking about the lavish gowns their mothers were creating for them a lump came to her throat as she realised there was absolutely no one to help her with this.

She so needed her mother.

ELLIE WAS FINISHING her homework when her father returned home from work and called his usual greeting to her as he walked into the living room. 'Hello darling, did you have a good day?'

She looked up at him and answered. 'Fine.'

'Hmm, so why do you look so glum?' he asked, frowning in concern.

'Sorry, Dad. It's just that there's this fancy-dress ball and everybody's going, and …well, I need a princess gown and…'

He smiled as he sat on the sofa next to her. 'Yes, I wondered when you would mention the ball, everyone is talking about it. And I see the problem.' He took her hand. 'But I tell you what Ellie, I have a friend at work, her name is Hillary, she is very good at making and creating. I'm sure she would help love, leave it with me.'

Ellie beamed at him with relief. 'Oh, do you think she will? Thank you so much Dad...and Dad?'

'Yes?'

'Do you ever think of mum?'

He squeezed her hand. 'My sweet little princess, your mother is somewhere in my thoughts every minute of every day. And I see her every time I see you. You have her smile and the same warm heart.'

Over the coming weeks Ellie often thought about the ball, imagining what her dress might look like. She spent many hours in front of her long mirror in her room, pretending to dance. One afternoon after school her reflective dream was interrupted by her phone ringing. It was her father.

'Hi dad.'

'Hey, princess, Hillary is coming for dinner tonight. Could you be a love and peel some potatoes? I'll sort the rest when I get home.'

'Who is Hillary?'

'The lady I told you about who's doing your dress.'

'Oh, of course. OK Dad'

'And Ellie, it's high time you met her anyway. You see,

there's no easy way to say this but… she and I have been seeing each other, and she is so eager to meet you.'

'What are you saying, Dad?' She felt panic rising up in her.

'Wait to meet her. I'm sure you'll get along famously. You'll see, Princess'.

When the call ended Ellie flopped onto her bed in disbelief at her father's words. Suddenly the ball disappeared from her mind and the gown she'd imagined became totally unimportant. She called Rose and sobbed into her phone.

'Oh, Rose. What am I going to do?'

'C'mon Ellie, it's not that bad! Your Dad was bound to meet someone, one day.'

'I suppose so, but what if I don't like her?'

'Look she's being kind enough to help you out with your dress for the ball, so she can't be that bad. Just get yourself ready and give her a chance.'

Wiping the tears from her face, Ellie made herself go down to the kitchen to prepare the potatoes and set the table. Once her chores were done, she glanced over at their ornamental biscuit container, which her mother had always loved and called "Bickie mouse". She tried not to cry again.

She went upstairs and rummaged through her wardrobe to find her smart black leggings and long red tunic. It was pretty and her mother had bought it for her. It was shapely, and with the leggings it complimented her slim figure. She sat on the edge of her bed in thought as she scrolled through her phone to see her messages.

An hour later she heard the front door open and ran downstairs.

'Ellie, you okay princess?' Her father walked in and gave her a hug as he draped his jacket onto the sofa.

'Erm, yes...'

A woman's voice spoke. 'Ellie how lovely to meet you. I've heard so much about you, dear.'

Ellie turned to see the woman who'd followed her father into the house.

'Princess, this is Hillary.' Jimmy loosened his tie as he spoke. Ellie took in Hillary's long brunette swept-back hair, forty-something appearance, and red lipstick complimenting a pretty smile. She saw Hillary admiring the room before she turned to Ellie with her hands on her hips.

'This is very quaint, I love it. Geraldine and Vicky would love this room.'

'Who are they?' asked Ellie anxiously.

Jimmy wandered over and put his arm across her shoulders. 'They are Hillary's

daughters, I should have told you; they're twins in fact, just a couple of years older than you.'

'They are wonderful, dear. I'm sure you'll get along.' Hillary added as she examined the candle holders before replacing them on the mantelpiece.

Ellie went down to the kitchen to check the table and to escape, but her father called her back. 'Come here, Princess. Hillary needs to take your measurements for your gown; I'll prepare dinner'.

Hillary was standing by the sofa with a tape measure. 'Ah, Ellie you would look adorable in light blue. I already have a design in mind for you, you will look amazing,'

'Thank you.' Ellie had mixed feelings, forcing a smile to her anxious face when they went downstairs to the kitchen to eat. She noticed her father's constant attentiveness to Hillary - who seemed nice, but something bugged Ellie. She couldn't help feeling something wasn't right.

'Hillary. Are Geraldine and Vicky going to the ball?' said Ellie as she forked some food into her mouth.

'Yes, although being a little older they're more grown up about it.' She giggled. 'Maybe they will both meet their prince, just like the fairy tales.'

'Oh, I see.' Feeling a little mocked by Hillary's words, Ellie looked at her father, but the mockery appeared to have gone unnoticed.

'I thought the weekend would be a good time to have Vicky and Geraldine round so you can all meet, princess, what do you say?' asked Jimmy as he started to clear the plates from the table.

'Good idea.' Hillary replied before Ellie could speak.

WHEN HILLARY LEFT Jimmy sat on the sofa and beckoned to Ellie to join him. 'Come here Ellie and sit with me a minute, I want you to tell me your thoughts.'

'Well I'm not sure, it's all so sudden.' She half stammered her answer as she perched on the edge of the sofa with her head hung in confusion.

'But isn't Hillary wonderful?' her father asked. 'I'll bet your gown will be outstanding; her kindness overwhelms me darling; she's the best.'

'Well I don't know her enough to say,' Ellie replied as she stood up from the sofa and faced him. 'But didn't you notice at dinner time how wonderful and grown up she says her daughters are, but I'm considered a small immature child?'

To her annoyance her father laughed. 'She didn't mean any harm by that. She was only saying they're already looking for Mr Right, whereas you…'

'Yeah,' Ellie interrupted. 'I'm just a kid who wants to play games of musical statues!'

'Ellie, don't be silly.'

'Leave me alone!' she shouted, as she stormed upstairs to her room and slammed her door shut.

Jimmy sat quietly for a minute then stood and wandered over to the mantelpiece. He picked up a picture of him and Maria, Ellie's mother, looking so happy together on their wedding day. 'Oh Maria, what would you say about all this? Am I doing the right thing? Is Hillary right for our baby girl?'

With a loud sigh he replaced the photograph and turned to go up the stairs to bed.

As the days passed. Ellie spent as much time as she could at Rose's house after school and dreaded the weekend with Hillary and her daughters.

'Rose, what do I say to them?' she asked her friend.

'I suppose hello would be a good start.'

'Rose, I'm serious.'

'Ellie, just be yourself, talk about the ball.' Rose handed her a can of Pepsi as they slouched on the armchairs, Rose's foot resting on the rim of the small coffee table in front of them.

'But…'

'Look, you might end up really liking them, Ellie.' she said as she sipped her drink.

'Hmmm.' muttered Ellie.

Rose stood up, grabbed her bag and rummaged through the change in her purse. 'C'mon, let's go into town and grab a pizza.'

Ellie shook her head. 'No, I'm going home. I don't feel hungry. I'm sorry.'

On her walk home through the neighbourhood, she heard a high-pitched meowing sound, like a pleading little cry. She moved in its direction, a bush to her left. Peering out from it was a tiny grey kitten. 'Oh, hello little fella.'

Ellie spoke gently as she picked him up, cradling him in her arms as he trembled with fear. 'Where is your Mummy?' She held him close to reassure him and carried him home.

Seeing him so lost reminded her of how she felt losing her mother.

'PLEASE CAN WE KEEP HIM? He is so lost. He needs a mummy.' she pleaded with her Dad when she got home.

'Well if no one claims him we can keep him, but you are responsible for him, caring for him and training him.' said Jimmy from the sofa as he looked up from his evening newspaper.

Ellie grinned at the kitten and her father in turn. 'Oh, thanks Dad. I am going to call him Gilbert.'

'Ha Ha! Hello Gilbert…' chuckled Jimmy as he got up and stroked the kitten's head and tickled his chin. 'It's nice to meet you'.

Little Gilbert brought smiles to Ellie's face all evening, as he played and clambered up the curtains. She knew they'd each found a new friend and a source of comfort.

THE WEEK FLEW by with Gilbert for company and before she knew it Hillary and her daughters arrived for their weekend visit.

'Well, well,' Geraldine said as she stood in front of Ellie looking at her from top to toe with a smug look on her face. 'I see why my mother feels so challenged creating your gown.' Ellie couldn't believe the spiteful words as Geraldine then admired herself in the long mirror in Ellie's room, looking proud as her small shapely figure reflected back at her.

'Yes, good point.' added Geraldine's sister Vicky as

they both looked around the room, smirking at Ellie's inexpensive trinkets and glaring at Gilbert curled up on the bed as they uttered words of sarcasm.

Ellie felt embarrassed and humiliated by how horrible they both were. She wished they would go and leave her to find solace with Gilbert, but she had dinner to endure with them.

As they sat in the kitchen round the table tucking into the roast dinner in front of them her father turned to both the sisters. 'So, girls. What do you think of Ellie's room?' he asked as he poured more gravy over his meal.

'Oh, it's so nice and little Gilbert is adorable.' answered Geraldine.

'And I love all her sweet little trinkets.' added Vicky as she wiped a strand of hair away from her face.

'No, that's not right!' Ellie said in disbelief at them lying to her father. This was a nightmare.

'What's that, princess?' he asked.

'Well…'

'Well nothing.' Hillary interrupted as she tucked into the final spoonful of her dessert. 'This is all so new, bound to be some teething troubles, right?'

'Yes, of course.' replied Jimmy, smiling at them all as he poured more tea for Hillary.

In her room later, Ellie propped herself up against her pillow and pondered on the latest negative situation which had unfolded in her life. And as they so often still did, tears welled up as she thought about her mother, and how much she wished she was here.

AT BREAKFAST the next morning Jimmy turned to her as he got the milk from the fridge.

'Look, I know this is all strange right now, but things

will get better, and I think the sooner they all live here, the sooner you will feel more settled…'

Ellie dropped the spoon into her bowl. She couldn't believe what she was hearing. 'But Dad, why…why would you want them to live here?' Her voice felt tight in her throat as she spoke.

'Because as I think you expected, I proposed to Hillary and she has accepted. There won't be a big do; we'll just go as a family to the registry office in two months where we'll tie the knot and….'

Ellie couldn't listen to any more. She ran upstairs in shock and slumped on the sofa. Jimmy followed her, crouched down in front of her, held her hand and spoke softly.

'Trust me, baby girl'.

Ellie gripped his hand and sobbed. 'Dad, I never expected this. You can't do it, they hate me!'

Her father stood and walked over to the mantelpiece, standing against it with his back to her and his hands in his pockets. His voice was firmer when he spoke.

'I know all this is hard, princess, but Hillary is right. For your sake we need to do this quickly, so you can move on.'

'No, you don't understand. And neither does she. She doesn't even like me!' she cried.

'On the contrary, Hillary has your best interests at heart darling. Oh, did she tell you she has nearly finished your gown?' he asked with a smile.

Ellie felt helpless as she muttered an 'Oh, right.'

As the weeks passed leading up to the wedding, her anxiety grew as she pleaded with her father to change his mind.

'Oh, Rose.' Ellie cried over the phone one evening as she sat on the sofa, her head resting against the cushion she was sharing with Gilbert. 'It's awful, my Dad can't see it, he just thinks I'm being unaccepting and awkward about everything.'

'I know it feels like a hopeless situation. But just see what happens. It might all get better.' Ellie knew her friend was trying her best to be reassuring.

The next day, as Ellie wandered through the town, she saw posters everywhere about the upcoming ball, but her excitement of it had been overshadowed by the turmoil caused by Hillary and her daughters. She stopped to window shop and admire some wonderful dance gowns, wishing one was hers, then turned to continue her journey home.

The lights were on inside the house as she walked up the path; she was greeted by her father and Hillary who waved her left hand at Ellie with delight, grinning at a shiny array of diamonds on a gold band.

Her father was beaming as he spoke. 'We did it, princess, we brought it forward. We thought it was for the best.'

Ellie couldn't speak. She stared at the ring and at Hillary, whose smug smile stared back at her. They walked into the house where Geraldine and Vicky greeted her with smug smiles.

'Welcome new sister.' they said in unison as Geraldine picked Gilbert up. Ellie reached for him, but Vicky blocked her path. 'He belongs to us now, ha!' she said as Geraldine swiftly carried the protesting kitten up the stairs. Ellie turned to appeal to her father, but she could see he was far too excited in his happiness of the day to notice anything remotely important to her.

Her father seemed oblivious to Ellie's torturing nightmare over the next weeks.

Her daily life was constantly shadowed in misery. The house was filled with false smiles and a pretended happiness. On the days her father was absent the constant mocking and sniping words from Geraldine, Vicky and Hillary got worse and Ellie felt like an outsider in her own home.

One evening, he was late arriving home. Ellie had escaped to her room, hoping he'd be back soon. When the doorbell shrilled, she walked down to the lounge to find two police officers talking to Hillary. When Ellie caught the end of the news they were breaking - that her father had been killed in a car accident that evening - Ellie broke down and screamed 'Why?' through loud sobs that wrenched her entire body.

She heard Hillary calmly address the policemen. 'Thank you. I know it's not easy delivering news like this.' As the officers nodded their sympathy and left, she turned to Ellie. 'Oh, stop your sniffling, you annoying child. Go to your room.' As Ellie started up the stairs, desperate to be alone with her grief, Hillary shouted after her. 'No child, you're going the wrong way; your sleeping bag is in the kitchen…'

'What do you mean?' asked Ellie as she turned on the stairs to face her.

'I mean that a servant's quarters are in the kitchen, so get your things and get down there and take your scrawny little cat with you.'

'You can't do this to me, this is my house.' Ellie shouted desperately through her tears.

Her stepmother just gave a high-pitched laugh. 'I think you will find this house is now mine. Your Dad rewrote his will last week. He knew I would care for you.' She laughed again.

'No, he wouldn't do that. And he wouldn't agree with this.' Ellie shouted louder, feeling distraught.

'Oh, just be quiet and get to the cellar where you

belong.' Hillary snorted sternly, standing at the top of the kitchen stairwell to usher her down.

ELLIE LAY on her sleeping bag, with blurred tear-stained eyes, then stood and wandered over to the Bickie mouse her mother had so adored and clutched it to her chest for comfort.

'Oh Mum.' she cried. She put the quaint container back on the counter and picked up Gilbert, who snuggled down with her in the sleeping bag. The sound of the clock ticking became fainter as she gradually drifted off to sleep. As she slept a magical drama unfolded before her.

She was sweeping the floor, when suddenly a voice caught her attention. 'Ellie, I am here to help.' Startled, she turned around to see a cute mouse standing on his two back legs. He was wearing a small top hat and tails and holding his hands in his pocket.

She gave him a quizzical look. 'Bickie Mouse?'

'Yep, that's right, it's me. I finally came to life, and I need to tell you to get a move on or you'll be late for the ball.'

'Am I going? Now?'

'Yes, you are, so get changed.'

She stammered. 'But…but I don't have a gown yet.' With that the little stoutly mouse grabbed the broom and twirled it around and as it turned a beautiful light blue gown swirled before Ellie's eyes. She put it on and danced round the kitchen in delight.

Then the mouse reached behind his back and held something sparkly out to her. 'Also, wear this mask; it's the rule of the ball. Yours is a Cinderella mask, it goes with your blonde hair'.

'Oh, but I can't get there!'

'Look out of the window.' said the mouse. 'Gilbert's taking you.'

A stunned Ellie looked outside and gasped as she saw a grey pony awaiting her. 'Oh Ellie.' The mouse's tone was serious.

'Yes?'

'This is important. Be back by midnight, and not one second later, otherwise your gown will turn back into a broom and Gilbert will become a cat again - but lost somewhere forever.'

Ellie's hand shot to her mouth. 'I understand. I shan't ever do anything to risk losing Gilbert'.

SHE CLAMBERED onto the pony which trotted her gallantly to the ball.

When she arrived, she marvelled at how many people were there; ladies and gents dressed in their finery danced around the floor joyously. As she watched a gentleman approached her dressed in a black suit and red bow tie. His mask was of a cat face which amused her as he spoke. 'Excuse me, young lady, may I have this dance?'

'Oh, yes'. Ellie smiled and hooked her arm through his as he escorted her to the dance floor.

'So, dream girl what's your name?' he asked as his strong masculine body moved her around with the music.

'My name is Ellie.'

He nodded. 'Ellie, nice name. And mine's Don'.

Ellie liked his name, and she already felt drawn to him, a mysterious stranger. His humorous but gentlemanly manner enthralled her, and they glided round the room with the feeling of magic between them.

When Ellie needed a break from dancing, he led her to the side of the room, and they talked. Don stared into her eyes through her mask. 'There's something special about you. I can't put my finger on it, but I would love to see you without your pretty princess mask. I need to see you again.'

Ellie's heart was pounding, but before she could answer, she saw the hands on the large wall clock clicked to ten minutes to midnight. In a panic Ellie shouted 'Sorry' and ran out of the hall, breaking the heel on her sparkly shoe in the process. Taking it off she clambered onto the pony barefoot and arrived home just as the clock sounded its final twelfth chime.

WHEN SHE WOKE up the next morning the reality of her situation hit her again, as she remembered her lovely dream. Gilbert was still snuggled bedside her and Bickie Mouse still rested on the kitchen counter.

Ellie's life was in tatters and the real ball never happened for her. Instead she endured the sheer delight of Geraldine and Vicky as they showed off the gowns their mother had created for them.

All Ellie had was a magical dream. She had no choice but to adjust to her new living arrangements, surrounded by the meanness of her horrible stepmother and wicked stepsisters.

But whenever she looked at Gilbert, she smiled at the memory of the dream they'd shared, and of Don - the mysterious stranger she'd magically met.

Two years later, and now eighteen, Ellie loved to escape the house when she could and walk through the village to the woods where she would pick flowers, as she used to when she was a child with her mother.

On a particularly lovely sunny day she picked too many and dropped some on the ground.

'Let me.' She turned as she heard the voice to find a

man in front of her; tall and slim, with short brown hair, he was wearing blue denim jeans and a white tee-shirt, and his muscular arms suggested he was strong.

'Oh, thank you.' said Ellie as he handed her the flowers.

Something seemed familiar about him as he replied. 'You're welcome, dream girl.' Ellie couldn't speak. All she could think of was her magical dream.

'Tell me your name.' he asked in a soft voice.

'Ellie, and you are?' Her heart was beating faster as she asked the question.

'Don.' he replied. 'Ellie, I think you are my dream girl.' He stared into her eyes as he spoke.

She stared back, transfixed by him. 'I think you have been in my dreams too.' He grinned at her. 'And this time I'm not letting you run away.'

THEY SPENT the following months texting, walking, holding hands and sharing their life stories and dreams. They spent evenings at their favourite Italian restaurant, laughing as they shared their strands of spaghetti until their lips clenched together at the middle with a kiss. There was a sense of magic between them.

Despite how bad things still were at home, Ellie began to sing as she did her chores. She couldn't disguise her happiness, which hugely annoyed Hillary and her stepsisters who were so intent on trying to keep her miserable.

One day Don arrived at the house asking to see Ellie. Vicky and Geraldine refused to let him in, but he pushed past them and went downstairs to the kitchen. The girls and Hillary followed him.

He ignored them as he took Ellie in his arms. 'Ellie, I love you, so much. Will you marry me?'

'What?' Vicky and Geraldine laughed in sarcastic unison. 'She is a trollope. If you want real class, it's us you should be looking at'.

Ellie ignored them and stood gazing lovingly into his eyes.

'Yes, I will marry you'.

Don swept her into his arms and lovingly kissed her. Then he turned to Hillary, Vicky and Geraldine. His voice was stern as he looked at them in turn. 'And as far as trollopes are concerned, three need to vacate this house now.'

'How dare you!' said Hillary. 'I'd like you to leave now, please.' Don ignored her and walked towards them waving some paperwork in front of their eyes.

'No. I don't think so. You see, I have here a copy of Jimmy's will. I'm a lawyer and I'm here to tell you this house has never been yours. You took advantage of a young vulnerable girl, who wouldn't know these things, but I do. This house belongs to her legally; you have no rights to it whatsoever, so get your belongings and leave now.'

'But that is preposterous! Where are we to go?' Hillary screamed and threw a spiteful glare at Ellie.

'Well,' said Don firmly. 'I'm sure you'll think of something. But I really don't care.'

Ellie stepped forward and touched his arm. 'Don, they have nowhere to go.' She turned to Hillary. 'You may stay Hillary, but only for three months while you find somewhere else to live. But we will be reorganising where everybody sleeps. We can discuss that later.'

Don looked lovingly at Ellie. 'You really do have the heart of angel.' He turned to the others and his face hardened. 'As for you ladies, you don't deserve any kindness, but I respect Ellie's decision. But you will receive an official letter stating the date you are to move out of here, is that clear?'

Hillary remained silent as she and her daughters turned in disgust to walk up the stairs. Don called after them. 'I suggest you buy two more sleeping bags for the duration of your stay here. I'm sure you'll agree the kitchen is the perfect place for servants…'

He put his arm around Ellie's waist, and she tried to stifle a giggle at the looks on her stepsisters' faces.

Six months later, Ellie felt at peace. She was happier than she could ever have dreamed possible as this long miserable chapter in her life had come to an end.

The weeks that followed the day of Don's proposal had flown by. Hillary, Geraldine and Vicky left, and Ellie at last got her beloved home back.

She and Don were married at the pretty village church, she wore a beautiful Princess gown, and Rose smiled all day as her bridesmaid.

Their reception was a fancy-dress ball in the evening, even grander than the one where their dreams had magically started.

And Ellie and Don lived happily ever after.

6

THE CHANGE

To the most special people who taught me right from wrong and gave me the strength to be the woman I am today; my parents, sadly missed and very much loved. And to my husband, who has been there for me through thick and thin; I would not be where I am today without his unconditional love.

by Jill Burgess

At twenty-eight, my life was plodding along predictably. Born, bred and still living in London, I enjoyed my job in advertising and adored my parents who had worked hard all their lives to give me a chance to have a good education and job. But recently I'd been edgy and restless; nothing felt quite right anymore. I needed a change; I couldn't keep looking into the future and seeing more of the same. I wanted some adventure in my life.

And now I was about to make the toughest decision I could imagine. I was an only child, so if I did what I was planning, Mum would be heartbroken.

I stared into my cup of coffee, as if it held the answers. *Where do I start? How do I break it to them?*

It had begun with Taylor of course. Our split after five years together had torn me apart; no man would ever compare to him. I'd thought our lives were mapped out and that happy ever after was guaranteed.

I asked my lukewarm cappuccino the question I'd asked myself over and over again. *What did I do wrong?*

He'd been my world, and I thought I was his - until 'that' day. My cup shook as the familiar pain shot through me. It still felt like yesterday - arriving at the flat and finding both of 'them' in the front room. Taylor almost choked at the shock of me turning up, then he'd stared down at the floor and said nothing. Ruby had stood in front of me, hands defiantly on her hips, and smirked as she proudly announced she was pregnant. Words crashed in a jumble into my head but got caught in my throat. My mouth refused to move.

Taylor had ushered Ruby out of the front door, whispering something in her ear. The gesture triggered my anger. As the man I thought had loved me stared back down at the floor again, as if he couldn't meet my gaze, the anger exploded.

'What the hell?! She was our friend! How, when, why?'

He looked up but I didn't wait for his reply. 'Get out Taylor. Now. Pack your bags and just go!!!'

As the door closed behind him, I threw myself on the sofa we'd bought together and shared so many times. And the tears flowed.

We never spoke or had contact from that day. I cried devastated tears for months. I thought they'd never stop.

Then one warm, perfectly British summer's day, I sat on my usual bench in the park for my lunch break, and it hit me - like a ton of bricks.

Poppy. If you don't do something with your life, you will end up a sad and lonely old lady!

And that was the moment my adventure started.

I waited till the weekend to tell my parents what I had planned. I'd already confided in my best friends; they'd all been encouraging and excited for me. But now I dreaded what my parents would say.

I arrived at the house I'd grown up in, and still loved, on Friday night after work. Dad cracked open our favourite wine and Mum had made my favourite dinner, her famous curry. Its spicy aroma filled the house with the familiar warmth and goodness that I always loved and associated with going home to Mum's cooking. After dinner and putting the world to rights as we finished the wine, I fell into bed in the early hours, but sleep was impossible. Tomorrow was the day, and I was dreading it.

I tossed and turned all night until I saw daylight and heard the birds tweeting. Stumbling downstairs clutching the sore head I deserved, I walked into the kitchen where Dad was whistling as he cooked bacon and eggs. The smell bought back childhood memories and I choked back a tear.

He turned and grinned at me. 'Morning Pops, you fancy a fry up?'

I forced a smile as I fought back tears that threatened to get the better of me at hearing my childhood nickname. 'Dad, you know I can never say no to your fry up. The best ever.'

'Hey sweetie, did you sleep well?' Mum was sitting at the table, giving me a quizzical look. She could sense something was wrong, and that there was a reason I'd come down this weekend. It was there in her eyes; she could read me like a book.

As we sat at the table, I knew I had to come out with it.

Here goes, I thought, looking down at my hands as I tried to find the words.

'Mum, Dad, I have to tell you something.' I looked up to see the alarm on my Dad's face and almost giggled. I'm sure he thought I was about to announce I was pregnant. Now I had no choice but to blurt out the truth.

'This is something I've been thinking about for a while now, and…it's difficult to tell you this, but…'

Mum put her hand on mine, when I paused. 'It's OK Poppy. Whatever it is, just tell us.'

I looked at them both in turn, then back down at the table before I spoke.

'I've decided to try life in Spain. I leave next month.'

There it was. I'd said the words. I looked up to see shock registered on both their faces and it seemed forever until Mum spoke.

'What? Poppy, why?'

Tears ran down my face. 'Please try to understand. I … I need a change to turn my life around. I've been unhappy for such a long time now, and haven't known what to do, but an opportunity's come up and I have to go for it.

Dad's questions came at me in a rush. 'But what will you do? Where will you go? Where will you live? How's any of this going to work?'

Now I'd got the news out I felt suddenly calmer. The practical questions I could deal with.

'I'm going to Seville. The teacher at my Spanish evening class gave me a contact there and I've been offered a job as a Tour Guide. So, I've packed my job in, here, and yesterday was my last day. I was never going to get any further in my career with the company. I need a new challenge.'

Dad's eyebrows knitted together. They always did when he frowned. 'I always thought you'd got yourself into a good firm here. Can't see this new thing paying much. How are you going to afford all this?'

'I've rented my flat out, so that should give me a fair amount to live on there. And please understand, this is not something I've just put together overnight. I've thought it through.'

Neither of them spoke for a moment. I could sense the emotion hanging in the air, filling the vacuum of silence.

I spoke into it. 'I would love you both to be happy for me. I'm not sure I can go if you can't. And I need to go.'

Without speaking they both stood up and hugged me so tight I could barely breathe.

Then Dad spoke. 'Pops, it's your life. You're a big girl now, you go for it. We're proud of what you've achieved so far, and we'll always be here for you, no matter what.'

I melted at his words. I loved my dad with all my heart; he had always been my rock.

Now the tears flowed. Tears of emotion, but of relief too that they now understood the secret I'd been carrying around for weeks.

I knew the news had shocked them, but we spent the rest of the weekend talking excitedly about my plans, planning when they'd come to visit me, and giggling about all times. When Sunday afternoon came, none of us wanted to face that it was time for me to leave.

As we said our tearful goodbyes, Mum pressed something in my hand and whispered in my ear. I knew she was suffering deep down, but she spoke with the wonderful calmness that had always been able to reassure me throughout my life.

'Open it when you get home. After you finish packing.'

'Oh, Mum, I love you.'

As I walked out of the door and pointed the alarm

remote at my car, I paused. *Was I really walking away? Could I do this?'*

Then I turned back to look at them both standing in the doorway, their arms around each other.

'I love you both with all my heart. I will be fine.'

AS THE PLANE began its final descent to Seville, and the seatbelt sign flashed on, my heart leapt with anticipation. My new beginning was less than twenty minutes away, but it felt like an eternity until the wheels hit the tarmac. Now my future was waiting for me on the other side of the aircraft's doors.

As I drove my hire car towards the city centre, I thought about Mum and Dad. The envelope my Mum had given to me had held enough cash to cover a few days' hire and I was already enjoying the freedom it gave me. I breathed in the magic of Spain and thought of the many childhood holidays I'd spent here. We'd visited various cities, including the one I was now speeding towards, as my parents had been determined for me to learn some of the culture as well as splash childishly in the pool. Maybe that was where my love for the country had started, and I felt its familiar magic cast its spell over me now.

In the centre of Seville, I met my contact Isabelle. We'd been communicating over social media for several months and already felt like friends, and she'd organised a small apartment for me which was cheap, but perfect. With my cases dropped off it was time for my first night in the city. As we ate seafood and drank Rioja, the vibe of the restaurant took me in - the noise, the chatter, the aroma of Spanish cuisine. I already felt at home.

In the early hours we left our final Flamenco bar of the

night and went our separate ways. I fell into bed exhausted.

I WOKE from a long and needed sleep, muggy and disoriented. Isa arrived with breakfast churros, the Spanish crispy version of doughnuts which we dunked in thick hot chocolate as we laughed together in both our languages. We'd hit it off from the moment we met online, and in person we found we had even more in common. We loved the same things and had the same aspirations for the future.

In between bites of her churros she spoke in her broken English. 'Today is Sunday, you come to the Campo with me to have lunch with my parents.'

'No, No. I don't want to intrude on your family time.' I replied.

'I insist, you no stay here alone.'

Part of me yearned to unpack and curl up on the sofa, but it was clearly not an invitation I could refuse.

I fell instantly in love with Isa's family home. Surrounded by olive and lemon trees in the heart of the Spanish countryside its setting was magical, and Isa's parents welcomed me as one of the family. Her parents spoke little English which forced me to practise my Spanish and led to lots of good-humoured laughter from us all when Isa explained some of my funnier mistakes.

'Oh, my brother is joining us later.' Isa suddenly blurted out.

'You never said you had a brother?' I was surprised she'd never mentioned him before.

'He is just back from working away. He spent six months in Thailand. Marco is an adventurer.'

A kindred spirit I thought.

Among Isa's extended family - aunts, uncles, cousins and grandparents who all arrived for lunch in traditional Spanish fashion - I felt at home. This was a culture of warmth and affection I could truly belong in, although I wished Mum and Dad could be there too and I looked forward to the day they would be.

We feasted on tapas of cheese and chorizo, followed by paella cooked by Isa's father; truly authentic. The best I had ever eaten and unlike anything I'd ever sampled in tourist restaurants.

Isa and I were preparing to wash a mountain of empty plates and dishes when I looked up. And there he was. I felt my jaw drop as I tried not to stare too obviously at the most handsome man I had ever seen. In a split second I knew all images and memories of Taylor had just been auto-erased from my brain's data bank.

'Hey sis, you did not say we had company.'

My body quivered and my insides melted at the accent which matched his looks. What was happening to me? A pair of smouldering deep green eyes, framed by long, jet black eye lashes were staring into mine. I could hardly speak as butterflies invaded my stomach. I extended a hand towards him, instantly feeling ridiculously British and over-formal.

'Hi, I'm Poppy.'

He smiled as he shook my hand. 'Hola, guapa. Encantado, estoy Marco.'

I was beaming inside; he'd called me good looking. And I'd fallen in love with his name. I imagined myself saying it and felt my cheeks flush at the thought.

That afternoon we chatted for hours, as if we had known each other for years.

I was enthralled by his stories of Thailand, and he took

time to listen to me too. I was almost frightened at how much I liked him already.

He told me that now he was back in Spain he'd decided to make his father happy by working alongside him in the swimming pool business he ran. Something his father wanted to pass on to him in the future. But he also told me travel was in his blood too, and I could sense he was not going to be around for long.

What was I thinking? I had only just started to get my life back on track and already this wonderful man was confusing it.

I fell comfortably into my job immediately; it was everything I'd dreamed it would be. Meeting different people from all over the world, joining them for dinner and introducing them to the non-tourist places the locals enjoyed - thanks to the rapid induction that Isa had given me.

Such a contrast from the days of being stuck in an office, staring at rain and miserable grey skies outside. I had loved my old job in London, but here in Seville life was colourful and vibrant. As the sun changed my skin from its usual pale to a healthy golden glow, and with happy people to make me smile, I felt my life had turned around. And it felt good.

Isa had become my closest friend and I found myself thinking less and less about the friends from home I'd been certain I'd miss. Now most of them only seemed to want me for the freebie holiday opportunity, but my friendship with Isa was different. She felt like the sister I'd never had. One day she said the one thing I'd been daring to hope I might hear.

'Marco has been asking about you more and more.'

I tried to look and sound casual, and to ignore the

fuzzy feeling inside at the mention of his name. 'Oh really?'

Isa just smiled and winked at me.

A FEW DAYS later he surprised me with a phone call out of the blue.'Hola chica. This is Marco.'

As if I could forget that accent, I stammered out a 'Hola.' in response.

In his near-perfect English he asked the question I'd hoped he would. 'Come to dinner with me tonight?'

Without hesitation I stammered out a 'Yes.'

By the time he picked me up at eight, I'd tried on ten outfits before finally deciding on a simple fitted dress in pale blue which Dad always said matched my eyes.

Marco was almost impossibly more handsome than I remembered. He took my hand as we walked to his favourite fish restaurant where he ordered the most delicious freshly caught seafood. We both kept smiling as we ate; we were in our element, certainly I knew I was. His eyes were the greenest of green, with the longest, darkest eye lashes I had ever seen. We talked non-stop throughout dinner - me in my still slightly London Spanish and Marco in his occasional broken English. Both laughing when we resorted to terrible Spanglish.

When Marco walked me home, I knew I didn't want this night to end. My flat was a mess, with discarded outfit choices strewn around, but I didn't care and invited him in anyway. We drank Rioja and talked until at 5a.m. when we both tipsily fell asleep on the sofa.

I woke up to find him staring intently at me as he pulled me closer and whispered into my ear. 'Poppy, do you know how much I am falling for you?'

'But we hardly know each other.' I whispered back as my heart skipped a beat.'

'I don't care, I just want to fall deep into every part of you.' he replied

'Let's not rush this Marco.'

He smiled the smile that melted my insides. 'I won't rush you, but I want to get to know you more and spend time with you. You make me feel whole in a way I've never felt before.'

I was on Cloud Nine. Could this really be happening? He pulled me close and kissed me tenderly on the lips. I kissed him back with a passion I hadn't known I possessed. I wanted every part of this man. In his arms I'd found life, love, happiness and the man of my dreams.

Life couldn't get any better.

7

BEGGARS CAN'T BE CHOOSERS

To my sister Rachel who introduced me to the fascinating world of fairy tales, has always encouraged me to pursue my writing and, is always there to support anything I do. And to Kayleigh who helped reignite my passion for writing and telling stories.

by Jenny Goodwin

In a quiet village, on an eerily silent street, sat a living corpse with cupped hands and feet tucked underneath for the tiniest hint of warmth. Threadbare rags draped the barely-there slip of a girl as the rain poured down around her. Much to the villagers' disdain, Gretel stayed in the same spot on the same road day after day. Nobles often travelled down this road, and after a long year of roaming all over the countryside, she found this spot to be the most favourable. Even now, at midnight in the downpour, she awaited a carriage with some elegantly dressed cargo and prayed that whoever was inside would take pity on her.

The famine had been hard for her. With not enough food and with deteriorating health, her mother had left this world. At only fourteen, Gretel had lost her house, her source of food and her only family in one fell swoop. At first, the church in her village took her in, fed her and cared for her. Then one night, as Gretel ate, her eyes drifted to the empty plate in front of the vicar at the other side of the table. Her food turned to sand in her mouth and she struggled to keep it down. The vicar smiled sadly at her; his eyes sunken into the rest of his face. She hadn't known he was giving up his food for her and she scolded herself for being so ignorant. Knowing she could not keep taking the vicar's food, Gretel said goodbye to the kind man and left with only the clothes on her back.

Once again, Gretel had no home and, like so many before her, became a vagrant. She never stayed in one place too long, especially after being chased out of several villages across the countryside.

As she gazed down the sodden road, she knew it was only a matter of time before this one turned on her too. Her eyes fluttered closed as she succumbed to exhaustion, oblivious to the sound of an approaching carriage's wheels as it rolled down the street. It rode so smoothly it would have appeared to be floating if anyone had been outside to watch it. Its passenger did not beckon the driver to slow down, but idly tossed a coin at the sleeping girl, without seeing if it had hit the intended target. Just as quickly as it had appeared, the silent carriage vanished into the rain and fog.

When Gretel woke, she blinked at the blurry street as her eyes adjusted to the unexpected sunshine. The material barely protecting her modesty was damp and she shivered against its clinginess, but her toes were beginning to tingle in the heat. A piercing shine penetrated her peripheral vision and she looked down at her lap to find a sparkling silver piece. Gretel thanked God for the kindness a stranger must have shown her while she was asleep. She slowly stretched out her aching joints and rose to her feet. Looking up, she noticed a curtain flicker in a window. She was used to being watched but, this time, she knew someone hoped she was leaving for good.

With her new found fortune, she headed towards the village square where the daily market would now be bustling with vendors and customers. Several people looked away as they saw her approach, not wanting to associate with the poor beggar child; others tutted and made rude remarks as she passed. Gretel knew from experience the stall holders would be picky about whether they served her; they didn't want the dirty beggar girl scaring off their important patrons. So, she headed to a more secluded section of the market, where many did not dare venture for fear of its associations with magic and witchcraft. The villagers didn't realise that there were still sellers with cloth and food among them.

Gretel laughed inwardly at the villagers' superstitions as they glanced suspiciously at the vendors on the outskirts of the village square. At a travelling seamstress's stall, she purchased a basic linen dress and short cloak which she changed into almost immediately, treasuring the smell and feel of new clothing. In the alley where she dressed, she tore her old clothing into small rags and plaited her hair, trying to gain some semblance of respectability. With only a couple of pennies left, she headed to the only food stall in this part of the market. An old woman with an arch in her back stood behind the table which was filled with every type of sweet and pastry; more than Gretel had ever seen before. After living such a dark and dreary life, she could barely comprehend the variety of colours on the table. She stood and gazed, transfixed by the delectable feast before her.

'How much is this?' she asked the old lady, as she pointed towards a pastry which was oozing a gelatinous substance.

'How much is what, deary?' The old woman's eyes darted around as her raspy voice struggled to get the words out. She held up a long, thin finger at them 'I cannot see, my child.'

'Oh. Sorry.' Gretel mumbled, 'I mean the pastry on your right.'

'Five coppers and it's yours.'

Gretel frowned at the only money she now possessed, 'I'm afraid I only have two.'

She watched warily and flinched as she felt the old lady stretched out a gnarled hand to touch her head. Bony fingers wormed their way down the side of her face and grazed one of the braids dangling over Gretel's shoulder. An overexaggerated smile twisted the woman's lips. 'I am not without conscience; I help those in need. It's yours for two.'

Gretel barely had time to contemplate how the woman knew she was desolate before she heard the hubbub of the market getting louder. She turned around to see the cause of the commotion and saw that several men had gathered in the centre, seemingly outraged at something. Gretel couldn't make out from her distance the source of their anger. Unable to look away she absentmindedly handed over her money to the old woman and simultaneously locked eyes with one of the men. Curiosity became dread as he raised his finger and directed his comrades towards Gretel. In moments, she was faced with a crowd of angry villagers. She didn't stop to thank the woman before she grabbed her purchase from the stall and ran from the village square.

She heard the heavy thuds of the men following her as

she raced down streets and through fields. Her shoeless feet darted to and fro as her slender build allowed her to race away from the threat. She'd known she would have to leave the village at some point but being physically chased out from somewhere was never Gretel's chosen method of moving on. She turned and headed towards the forest, hoping she could hide and be safe under the dense cover of the trees. By the time she reached the edge of the woods and looked back, the men were tiny dots along the horizon; still pursuing her, but slowly.

She scrambled her way up one of the trees and found a limb strong enough to support her. As she settled into the safety of the nook, Gretel realised she had overestimated the strength of her body against the chase she'd endured. Her heart pounded in her chest as if it might explode and her thighs burned as if they'd been set alight. She used her hiding place to catch her breath and recover and from her vantage point could see the men stumble through the underbrush searching for her. She sat and waited, breathing as quietly as her pounding heart allowed until the sun began to melt behind the treetops.

'It's almost sundown, we must go back. She is long gone by now.' Gretel heard one of the men say. 'Besides, we do not want to be entangled with the witch as after dark.'

Gretel gave a quiet scoff at their superstitions as she watched them leave. Relief as her heart stopped pounding was replaced by a grumble from her stomach as a delicious smell pervaded her nose. Slightly crushed in her hand, and almost forgotten, it was from her pastry. It seemed larger than it had on the stall - much larger than her average meal – but without pausing between mouthfuls Gretel gobbled the entire thing up. Her taste buds danced at the unique, fruitful flavours of the filling which slowly trickled from her mouth. She licked up every drop, enjoying eating something other than her usual diet of stale bread.

Pastry demolished, Gretel nestled into the crook of her tree's limb, ready for a night's sleep. The satisfying aftertaste of the pastry, and a full stomach for once, lulled her into a deep, dreamless sleep.

NEARBY IN THE SAME FOREST, but unseen by Gretel, a cottage swayed in the breeze. Its wooden structure was old and rotting and the roof leaked so much that the family within had no more pots to cook food in. Ignoring the whistles coming through the walls and the creaking of the floors, a young boy, barely thirteen, laid his head on the hay mattress in the cupboard. His eyes had barely closed when he heard raised voices.

'We are going to starve!' A woman's shriek pierced his ears. His stepmother.

'No, we will not!' His father asserted. 'Stop shouting or you'll wake him and scare him. All we need to do is ration more.'

'That's still not going to feed all three of us! You know what we have to do.' Hansel's breath stopped as he listened in fear to his stepmother's screaming. He knew what came next. 'The boy has to go.'

He didn't hear his father's reply, nor did he want to. He knew his father would give in, just like last time. Hansel knew there was no food and he was old enough now to comprehend the concept of a famine, and how there was no food anywhere. Three years ago, when the last nationwide hunger had struck, his stepmother had convinced his father to abandon him in the woods. Hansel had been smart then, he had unlocked the back door and used pebbles to guide him home.

And when he'd checked earlier this evening, the back door was locked and bolted. His stepmother did not want him back again. Hansel closed his eyes and tried to sleep as best he could; he knew he would need all his strength tomorrow.

He awoke to the growls of his stomach, louder than normal from a combination of both hunger and trepidation. He lay still, allowing his eyes to adjust to the four small walls of his nook which smelled like a mixture of fresh wood and sweat. It was dark, with no windows, but at least it gave him some privacy. With only two rooms, their small woodcutter's cottage barely housed the three of them. His father's voice calling him for breakfast roused Hansel from his thoughts. He rolled up his mattress and awkwardly dressed himself, with a hunched back and elbows banging on the walls.

'Good morning son.' His father said as Hansel emerged from the cupboard. 'Here, eat up.'

Hansel took the wooden plate from his father and stared sadly down at the half slice of bread, but he quickly wiped the frown from his face as he sat down. 'Thank you, Papa.'

His father took the chair opposite him with a sad look in his eyes. 'I thought you could join me today. I need some help carting the wood back.'

This was the same conversation Hansel remembered from three years ago, but he nodded. As soon as his father went outside to fetch his axe, Hansel stuffed the bread into his pocket – it would be his only hope again of finding his way back to the cottage from the depths of the forest. His father didn't question its sudden disappearance and the two set off together. They didn't venture too far, and to Hansel's relief he could still see the cottage from where they set to work.

The day began like any other; his father chopped the trees and Hansel put the small logs into the cart. His father sang and seemed so cheerful that Hansel almost forgot the conversation he had heard the night before, hoping that his father had changed his mind. But sadly not. At around midday, his father spoke the words that Hansel didn't want to hear.

'I need you to go deeper into the forest and find a tree with a sizeable trunk that will produce enough wood to construct a wall of a house. Once you have found it, mark it and we will return tomorrow. I will take the cart back to the house and I will fetch you at sundown.' As he spoke, his father hammered a post of wood into the ground to mark the spot and to be used to keep time.

Hansel knew there was no such tree and he also knew that his father would not return. And as he watched his only family walk away from him, the knot in his stomach grew bigger. Dragging his feet, he did as his father ordered; he still possessed some childlike naivety and prayed his father would indeed come searching for him and not listen to his wife.

But as he walked, he picked off pieces of bread and scattered them on the ground behind him. The bread soon ran out and Hansel stopped walking to settle down and wait until his father, hopefully, returned. He slumped against the base of a tree and watched the birds fly from treetop to treetop. Afternoon soon turned to evening which eventually led to sundown coming and going without a sign of his father. The boy began to weep silently as realisation set in that he was on his own.

Up until this point, he'd nursed a slight glimmer of hope that his father would still come back for him, but now he cried until his exhausted head fell against the tree trunk and his eyes matted shut with his tears.

Unknown to him, a young girl sitting in the nook of a tree had been silently watching him and had seen the crows eat all the crumbs from the floor. She had wanted the crumbs for herself and cursed the birds who got to them before her. She had just eaten her first meal in four days and craved more as another sweet smell entering her nose only got stronger and stronger.

As the sun rose above the trees, Hansel wiped the crust of matted tears from his eyes. He scolded himself for spending the previous night weeping like a child. He was, after all, almost a man and should begin acting like one. In his heart of hearts, he knew what he would see when he turned to check on his bread trail but a part of him still wished that God had spared him yet another heartache. He turned to check the trail and sure enough, every morsel had been devoured, leaving him with no way of guiding himself back home. Sighing, he pushed himself away from the tree and tried to walk back home. However, Hansel did not know the forest like his father did and was taking a direction that headed deeper into the forest. He did not know he'd been watched and was now being followed. In the shadows, a girl studied the young boy, a feeling of sympathy burrowing itself into her chest. She knew what it was like to be alone in the world, to have everything taken away. She wanted to help this poor boy, but she also knew he was guiding her towards more food, as with every step he took, the aroma that seemed to engulf the entire forest got stronger. The same scent that had stayed with this girl since she had eaten the pastry in the tree.

As evening began to settle in, and as he thought his legs would give up on him, Hansel stumbled on a small house in a clearing. It was a sweet house; wooden with ivy climbing up its walls. Freshly baked goods sat on the windowsill, steam drifting upwards and entering his nose.

Behind him, Gretel's nose also twitched at the smell. She breathed deeper and deeper, allowing herself to be enticed by the delicious aroma. Her foot involuntarily moved forwards, and only stopped short when she saw Hansel take small, shaky steps towards the house. This distraction was enough to clear Gretel's head. Something didn't sit right here. The house seemed too homely and the smell was so sweet, it was almost sickly.

Hansel got closer to the window sill, and reached out his hand to grab a warm pie, shoving it whole directly into his drooling mouth. Gretel started to move out from behind the tree to warn him; to tell Hansel to run away. But she was too late. The front door of the house creaked slowly open to reveal an old woman with an arch in her back. The woman's eyes darted around, not quite focusing on her unexpected visitor. Gretel recognised the woman a moment too late as a familiar raspy voice filled the clearing.

'Who do we have here?' The woman stretched out an arm and long, bony fingers entangled themselves in Hansel's hair. The outstretched fingers began to make their way down the head until they found nothing but air. 'Not who I was expecting... but beggars can't be choosers. Why don't you come in for a bite?'

Gretel's eyes followed Hansel as he accepted the hag's offer and stepped over the threshold. A sinking feeling started deep in her stomach as the pieces all fell into place; she knew who the old woman had been waiting for. Gretel turned and ran away from the all-too-precious food and the old lady.

And, for the moment, from a boy, but she knew at some point she would go back. Their story wasn't over. At some point he would need her help.

8

BECAUSE I'VE LOVED HER MANY TIMES BEFORE

To Dean, for being the inspiration I never knew I needed, and so much more.

by Reef Pearson

She threw herself onto the beat-down sofa in the middle of the staff room, sweeping her hair over the cushions behind her with both hands as she sunk her head back. I admired her as she stared at the ceiling, eyes fixated on the blank canvas as if projecting her thoughts onto it in an attempt to organise them. I studied her as she teased the end of her unlit cigarette around her lips. It was the most deliberately sultry motion I imagined a woman could achieve without taking her clothes off, but her distant eyes suggested she was too fixated on other thoughts to make her allure anything but serendipitous. She was a vision.

I cautiously sat down in the chesterfield armchair opposite her, leaning back into the cracked leather, worn down in that clichéd 'old bar way' where the foam inside is exposed by gaping flaps of fabric caused by years of disrespectful drunken use. I stretched my legs out and casually landed them on the coffee table that separated us; a probably too obvious attempt to appear more relaxed than I felt.

Her phone was precariously placed next to a pool of flat beer beside my feet, and my eyes drifted to it as it lit-up once again. I knew it was fast-approaching the time that she'd have to confront the build-up of missed calls and texts that I'd been complicit in pretending hadn't been coming through for the past hour.

I spread my thumb and forefinger idly across my mouth, trying to maintain a poker face as I gazed at her, evaluating the damage that our radical passion had incurred. Her blouse was a little more crumpled than when she first entered the bar, her hair with a few more wispy fly-aways, and her make-up smudged where my hands had grasped her face only a few moments ago. Her lips parted to the sound of a short inhale as she broke the silence.

'I'm sorry, Owen.'

I retracted my legs from their outstretched position and leaned forward, resting each elbow on its coordinating knee. 'Jess, don't ever apologise for exercising your right to say no to a man.'

She responded to the bait I'd just set out for her with a look that danced along the fine line between a giggle and a smirk. Mimicking my stance, she leaned forward into me and flicked the less-than-tasteful lighter with the hula girl in an 'asset-accentuating' coconut bra, bringing its flame to the cigarette now pursed between her lips. Her eyes locked with mine as she blew out a cloud of hazy smoke in a gesture that was as flirtatious as it was patronising.

'Insecurity isn't a colour that looks good on you, Owen,

and I'm not a girl who needs her human rights explained to her by a half-cut man in *Ziggy's* staff room. Just to state the painstakingly obvious, the unfortunately sorry thing about us is that we both wanted it as much as each other. We always do.' She shook her head and upturned the corners of her mouth, which highlighted the playfulness in her words.

I raised my eyebrows and touched the tip of my tongue to my top lip. Her statement warranted applause more than it did an immediate response. The more she taunted me, and us both, the more I felt myself melting into her - ever more aware that if we both leaned in a few more inches across the table we would be enthralled in each other once again.

'How much longer are we going to pretend that Alice doesn't exist?' Her question was loaded with shattering disenchantment.

'Don't do this Jess.' I heard the pleading in my own voice.

'Owen, she's pregnant.'

As if I didn't know, but those words are still like a punch in the teeth every time I hear them. Despite my body telling me to hurl my beer across the room, I take a sip and bend to place it on the floor next to me, an action calculated to buy precious time to compose myself.

MY THOUGHTS FLASH TO ALICE, a silhouette of a ghost, the ultimate convenient comforter after a 4a.m. bar close and too many short drinks.

'What's the harm in a little fun?' had been her assured *WhatsApp* sales pitch when the clock had ticked into the early hours of Sunday morning. Alice's intentions were always transparent to me. She seduces you to feed her own ego, and with a face like hers, it's easy to comply. But she's the type of girl whose desperation radiates off her. A pretty face loses value when you're suffocated by her constant need for you to validate it.

Spending a night with Alice promises much, but comes with the predictability that when daylight arrives, you'll remain entirely unfulfilled. It doesn't take long to conclude she's the type of girl who isn't worth it.

She is incomparable to Jess in a way that words can't capture. Through gritted teeth, I said for what felt like the hundredth time. 'I cannot force a woman to take a morning-after pill; I said my piece, but her body is her own.'

Jess stared through me with wide distant eyes, biting the inside of her cheeks until she appeared skeletal. Her thought-process was almost audible as I sensed she held back what she really wanted to say and scrambled to replace the words with something more 'morally-correct'. In the years I've known Jess I've developed a knack of translating her facial expressions into their own infinite language, and this face of defeat was one that I recognised all too well.

In an attempt to spare us both some protracted painful to-and-fro dialogue, I cut to the chase. 'Jessie, why did you come to the bar tonight?'

She spun herself around on the battered sofa and flicked her legs out lengthways across it, causing her skirt to rise higher up her thigh - challenging my illusion that I couldn't physically feel any more lust towards this woman.

'Well, I always come to see you at work the night I'm back in town.' she said in a confident fashion that contradicted every reason we weren't making love again this very second.

I leaned forward to reply, swiping a Marlboro from the near-empty packet that she'd carelessly tossed on the table next to the beer puddle. 'Take me then. If that's all you came here for.'

With tantalising slowness, Jess put her hand into her pocket and pulled out the hula girl lighter. With one arm outstretched, she leaned across the table and lit the cigarette hanging between my chapped lips. I tipped my head back, eyes closed in a fleeting blissful moment until I felt a sharp sting to my right cheek and my cigarette flew to the floor from the shock of the slap.

My body stiffened. I opened my eyes and stared at the slowly burning Marlboro on the floor, then at the empty battered sofa as I heard the door close behind her.

My brain swam with a frenzy of competing thoughts as I sat on the night bus home, empty at 5a.m. apart from a group of 18-year olds in crop tops groping each other and eating kebabs.

I thought about Jess. Every time she comes back from London, I get so entangled in my infatuation for her that I forget that even she is not perfect. Because I only get to see her for a few short days every couple of months, during her absences I file her in an impenetrable bubble in my mind where I can't see her as anything less than a dream.

But I believe that relationships require tolerance and while all good relationships inevitably encounter intolerances, you should never raise a hand to the one you love. And no matter how much she exhilarates me, when I'm with Jess I'm constantly aware that the height of the highs usually descends to the low of the lows, so basically you get screwed either way. We'll laugh at everything either of us has to say while being hyper-aware of every time one body even merely grazes the other.

I constantly want to grab her and kiss her as if we're on a passionate one-night-stand, but I don't want it to be a one-night-stand at all.

Then inevitably, she leaves again.

AS I HEAD up the hill towards my flat the familiarities of my post-work walk from the bus stop consume me. Faulty porch lights flicker as my motion disturbs them when I pass; the parked cars that shade my footing from the dim light of the street lamps force me to focus on my steps.

I pause to light a cigarette as I pass the rose bush. Trial and error have taught me that if I light-up here then I can neatly finish my smoke in the time it takes for me to walk from this point to my front door without having to finish it in the cold before I go inside.

AND THAT'S when I saw her, lingering outside, her familiar figure perched on the low brick wall with her legs crossed over in front of her, signature Marlboro in her hand.

'Owen!' she yelled.

She sounded drunk. I quickened my pace and threw my unfinished cigarette into the gutter, momentarily irritated at wasting it. I pulled her up off the wall which took more effort than if she'd been sober. She fell into me and kissed me.

'What the hell are you doing Alice?'

She slurred a taunting reply. 'What we do every Saturday night Owen...'

Was this a cruel joke? I pulled her inside, hoisting her up the stairs as though this was any other drunken Sunday morning to be regretted later. She flung herself on the sofa and flopped like a ragdoll. Blood rushed to my head as I looked at her. What was she doing drinking in her condition?

I glared at her. 'The baby Alice! You're drunk. What about the baby?!'

She shook her head as tears streamed down her face, leaking mascara from her eyes like a grey curtain across her face. 'There never was a baby.'

I grabbed her shoulder and spun her far-too-aggressively to face me, my own face scarlet with anger. 'What the hell are you saying?'

She stuttered through her hysteria. 'There's no baby. I just needed a place to stay, for a while. I…I was going to say I'd lost it soon. I didn't know what else to do. Owen, please, try to understand. I was desperate.'

I left the flat as abruptly as my woozy legs would allow, closing the door on Alice's sobbing, eager to escape and be alone. I stood on the street and looked up at the flat's window. My stomach churned with disgust; I felt used. What a situation to put a man in.

Then I looked up again, thought of Alice's tear-stained face, and felt sorry - for her and for me. For her to have been that drunk at god-knows-what-time on a Sunday morning; to have shown up at her fake baby's dad's flat because she had nowhere else to go - I felt overwhelmingly sad for her. Empathy overtook my anger. No matter how much I was hurting because I'd been manipulated, there was a girl upstairs in hysterics because she was paying for a decision she'd felt she had no choice but to make.

I LIT another cigarette and checked my phone. There it was, 'Jess 05:34 - *Can I come over?*'.

My grip weakened as I read the message. My chest tightened as I took a long draw of my cigarette. Then I exhaled smoke and my finger trembled as I deleted the message and glided my phone back into the pocket of my jeans as though it was the most fragile possession I owned.

I couldn't do it; I can't do it. This decision was not an easy one. I've loved her many times before and I could love her for a lifetime more. But right now, someone really needed me, and it wasn't her.

It never was her.

9

EVERYDAY VIOLET

I wrote this story as a single woman who lives alone during the 2020 lockdown, knowing that my experiences were different to a lot of my peers and other people in the lockdown situation because of my marital status. As a frustrated writer, who has always talked herself out of actually putting pen to paper (or fingers to keyboard) this was the perfect opportunity to spend some time with my own thoughts and try and craft something that others might relate to. I hope you enjoy reading my story and all the other stories in our collection.

by Laura Fell

Every day, Violet (aged 39 years and 364 days) follows the same routine.

She sets her alarm for exactly 7.10am and allows herself a snooze of an equally exact nine minutes. She then reaches for the remote control from her bedside table and turns her TV on to watch the news and find out what's been happening in the world while she's been sleeping. It's usually not the best start to the day.

She then (usually with a slight groan) prises herself out

of bed and walks, or rather meanders, to the bathroom. Her right knee always clicks through the first steps of the day. She places the bathmat on the floor by the side of the bath, pulls the shower curtain across and lets the water from the shower head warm through.

Today is Monday morning, which means hair-washing day. The usual weekly routine for haircare is every other morning for hair washing - unless exercise has been involved, or it's been a hot day, which means a shower including a hair wash is the only way to feel comfortable before getting into bed. She prefers non hair-wash mornings - there's less rushing to complete the rest of her routine.

After today's shower, which includes the treat of a body scrub - *well why not start the week off well?* - she examines her face in the mirror. Her pores are large, her skin has red patches, she has dark circles under her eyes, and she needs her upper lip waxed. She decides her hairline is too close to her eyebrows on the side of her face. She thinks her lips are getting thinner as she gets older.

She frowns about how imperfect her face is and has always been, then realises the frown does nothing to enhance it. She also realises she can't remember the last time anyone else was physically close enough to see the imperfections she sees. She then thinks about the fact she turns forty tomorrow.

40 - the two numerals are all her eyes can see. When she was a child, forty was ancient; when you were a teenager it was your Mum's age. But Violet didn't feel forty, and she didn't feel the way she'd expected forty would feel. She didn't feel old. She didn't really feel much at all.

She wonders whether anyone else would even notice these imperfections. Surely people look for expressions and for a connection; they don't look to criticise.

Well, she thinks, *that's how I look at other people anyway*.

She hopes she gets the same in return from others. Then she decides she can't let the thought of what might, or might not, go through other people's heads when they look at her stop her getting ready for work and leaving her flat on time.

She cleanses and tones her face the way her beauty bible says she should, and then moisturises. She notices that today the moisturiser is absorbed more quickly than usual. Maybe her skin needs a bit more attention after the two runs she did over the weekend. *I'll wear sunscreen tomorrow*, she thinks.

Or maybe she's just turning 40, she thinks.

She rarely uses what her beauty bible calls a 'full' face of makeup. Instead she uses tinted moisturizer, makes her eyebrows look a bit fuller and applies one coat of mascara. It takes her five minutes.

Job done, she opens her wardrobe. What to wear today? Luckily her workplace is casual, so she opts for her favourite indigo blue jeans (artfully ripped on the right knee), and a smart-ish high-necked blouse with a red, blue and cream lined pattern on it. The sales assistant had told her those colours flattered her colouring.

As her weight has slowly crept up over the past couple of years, she's now comfortably in the curvy range, and it's rare she finds something that she feels truly comfortable in – but this is a comfy outfit.

So, she's starting the day off with washed hair, one of her favourite tops and a comfy pair of shoes. She accessorises with a statement necklace as a finishing touch.

Yes, she thinks, *today will be a good day* – at least by Monday's standards.

. . .

SHE CHECKS THE TIME; she only has ten minutes to check she has everything for the day. Today will be a breakfast-on-the-go day. She grabs her work bag and does a quick check of the contents. Purse, notebook, phone charger, water bottle. All present and correct. Apart from one thing. She picks up her reusable bamboo coffee cup, that has a detachable cup holder to prevent heat escaping. The cup holder has 'You've got this Violet' written on it.

Yes, she thinks, *today, Violet, you do*.

As she opens the front door to her flat, she pauses - doing one last mental check that she's covered everything in her everyday routine, which also includes this everyday final check.

Satisfied, she closes the door behind her, and locks it. She pushes the door gently, just to make sure it's definitely locked. She smiles as she does it. She thinks there hasn't been a single time in the three years she's lived in here where this hasn't happened every time she's left the flat. That little door push had become part of her everyday routine too.

She walks the twelve-minute walk to the train station and looks at her watch three times to make sure that she'll definitely make the train comfortably, and her pace is on track. It is.

She taps her pay-as-you-go Oyster Travelcard onto the reader and checks the balance. She'll be fine for this week and won't need to top up until next Monday. *Great*, she thinks to herself. *A straightforward journey to work*.

In fact, a straightforward Monday morning generally, so far.

But as she steps up onto the train, she steels herself with a deep breath – this is where the day actually begins. Socialising. Making an effort to be around other people.

She spends so much time by herself that she's used to

her own company. After a weekend of it, Mondays were always an adjustment. Violet tells herself she enjoys being alone and likes being self-sufficient. She doesn't let herself think about any alternatives or imagine any parallel lives she might have lived had she made different choices - or had other people not made choices for her.

She looks around for an empty seat. Suddenly all around her she sees couples. There's a married couple so clearly in sync with each other that they don't even look up from their respective reading materials to pass a shared cup of coffee between them. There's a seat free opposite them. She considers that as the last resort.

There's another young couple who are chatting away. She tries not to tune into what they're discussing because it feels like she's intruding. She decides to move away from them too; suddenly she's not in the mood to hear excited voices talking about their loved-up weekend and their plans for the week ahead.

Of course, she doesn't need these avoidance tactics when she's on her own, in her own flat, in her own routine, with everything ordered just as it should be. There she feels strong, independent, powerful. She knows that no matter what life throws at her she can face it. There's a sense of pride in her routine and the fact that she doesn't need anyone. Everyone in her life is there through invitation and she's comfortable with that.

She's never felt the biological need to have a child even though she loves children. When she gets invited to a wedding with a plus one, she knows it's a courtesy – nobody expects her to bring anyone. She jokes about there being no eligible men in London and she jokes about people with baggage looking for love. She's worked hard to make sure she's still interesting and relevant to her friends, as one by one they all found partners and had children.

But for some reason, this morning feels different. Something felt changed.

What did she have to show for her life? To show for twenty years of working? To show for twenty-two years minus one day of being an adult? She was single and childless. Did anything else matter?

She finally took a seat next to someone who didn't move to give her enough room to be comfortable, opposite a man who was biting his fingernails, and a young blonde woman with the hugest diamond ring she'd ever seen on her wedding finger.

Violet's mind was racing. Her heart was pounding in her chest and she felt light-headed. Was she going to faint?

*Deep breaths...*she told herself. *Deep breaths...*

The train had gone through two stops by the time she got herself focused. She always did in the end, but it had taken longer today.

Why had that happened?

Here she was - successful, ambitious and independent; liked, respected and healthy. Whatever that wobble was, it was a temporary blip. Something to be overcome; something she would forget about as she powered through today and into tomorrow.

Tomorrow... there would be cards and a cake, and people singing Happy Birthday to her out of tune. She hated a fuss; she'd better start mentally preparing herself for it. She felt the wobble returning.

Deep breaths...

Focus...

But her mind flashed to Andy. The ex-boyfriend who she had met at thirty and 4had thought she would marry and have children with. She thought of the flat they'd shared in South London; how it had been her favourite place in the world with her favourite person in the world.

She had felt so happy then. She remembered them setting off in her Clio on road trips to see friends, of meeting up after work for dinner before heading home.

And she thought of the emptiness she'd felt when he left. The sick feeling that had pervaded her every waking minute of each day that followed. The tears she'd thought would never stop when he said he thought they would be better as friends.

And the deepest cut of all - the photo she had seen of him with his wife and baby daughter when a mutual friend on Facebook had posted it. She felt the pain of that cut even now - sitting on this train on a random Monday morning, six years later.

Six years that had gone by so quickly. *What did she really have to show for them?*

Stop it. Focus on the good stuff Violet. Deep breaths...

She thought of Ben. He'd been completely in love with her and had wanted her to move in with him -forever he'd said. She tried not to think about his hurt expression when she'd told him that she didn't see that with him, that it would never happen.

Because she couldn't get past Andy. And her head still refused to let him go. She tried not to see that photo of his child and wife.

Instead she thought of the multiple first dates she'd had over the years. All lovely guys, most of whom she didn't remember any details about - apart from the recurring stomach-sinking realisation with each of them that once again this wasn't going to be love.

Love. Had she ever truly loved and been loved in return?

That's all she'd wanted really. For someone to feel what she felt, someone to want what she had wanted.

She thought about how it had been two years since she'd even had a date.

Deep breaths…

She silently repeated the mantras she'd prepared for whenever she felt overwhelmed like this.

'What's happened to you has made you the person you are.'

'You are not half a person because you're single; you are already whole.'

'If someone can't compliment you and make you feel worthy and valued, they're not worth having in your life.'

'Don't ever settle.'

'Don't let yourself wake up next to someone every morning and just tolerate them.'

'You have everything you need in your life.'

'Life is not and will never be, a fairy tale'.

Focus…Deep breaths…

THE MANTRAS WORKED and calmness returned. She knew she was OK. She knew she'd make herself stay OK. Or OK enough at least.

The breeze from the open train window hit her face and added some reassuring coolness to the calmness.

Her life was fine as it was. She didn't need a partner, boyfriend, husband, child to validate herself.

She was Violet, and she was approaching the penultimate stop of her journey; she was ready for her week to begin. She watched London pass by through the train window. Her mouth tilted in a slight smile as she thought again about turning forty tomorrow. Cards, cake and singing - surrounded by people who loved her. She wondered if they would put candles on the cake.

Deep breaths…

'Excuse me, is this seat taken?' Violet turned her head in the direction of the question and stared - speechless – into the eyes that met hers and stared speechlessly back.

She found her voice and stammered a reply. 'Yes, of course.' Her hand flew up to her cheeks as she felt herself blush at the expression the handsome man in front of her wore. An expression that made her feel she was the most interesting object on earth.

'I'm Craig.' he said.

She reached out to shake the hand he offered. 'I'm Violet.'

And she smiled, because something inside her knew. This was no longer a random, 'everyday' Monday; this was going to be a good day.

And as Craig held her hand as if he didn't want to let go, she had a feeling tomorrow would be a good day too. There would be lots of good days ahead.

And she wouldn't even count the candles on her cake tomorrow.

10

RED AND THE WOLF

To my family, for always supporting my creative outlets.

by Kayleigh Hunter

'BEAUTY MEETS BEAST MAGAZINE'

Everyone knows the story of Little Red Riding Hood. A little girl goes to see her grandmother and they both get devoured by a wolf, and depending which ending you read, they were either saved by a hunter or they weren't. A pretty grim tale; Brothers Grimm to be precise.

But here at BEAUTY MEETS BEAST we wanted to learn the truth behind the fairy story, so after much digging and research we finally found the real Miss Riding-Hood herself. When asked, she was more than happy to be interviewed and to give us her story, the real story. This is what she told us: -

"PEOPLE THINK, because it says little in the title, that I was nothing more than a child, but I wasn't.

And the story the Brothers Grimm wrote does have some truth to the actual story, but only some. Yes, I went to spend time with my grandmother; and yes, a hunter was involved, but not in the way they portrayed it.

It all started the week of my sixteenth birthday.

Where I come from it is a tradition that the young ladies of our community are celebrated coming into womanhood; this is when the young ladies come into their sixteenth year. The celebration lasts for four days, and it starts with a blessing from the eldest member of each young lady's family. For me, that was my grandmother.

I didn't have a big family, but it was a loving one. I lived with my mother and stepfather and my grandmother only lived a short distance from our house. Getting to it did mean walking through the woods, but then all the best locations to live tend to involve a trail through the woods. On the day of my birthday I was told to take some important items for the blessing, so in a basket my mother packed a white silk dress, a red ribbon and a blue pendant, along with enough fresh flowers to make a crown and some sweetmeats and breads. The dress represented innocence, the red ribbon change, and the blue pendant peace of self and mind going forward.

Clutching my basket, I set off to spend time with my grandmother. I was to spend two nights with her before moving to the next stage which was a cleansing before the ceremony. I am a little sad to say this tradition no longer exists now, as young people of today see it as vulgar, sexist nonsense. But, at that time, being pure meant that you would be selected to become a bride to the most eligible bachelors of the community; young men who were no older than yourself.

For us girls it was an exciting time, for we got to wear a pretty frock, have sweet treats and dance. Maybe if we were lucky, we also got to have a romance with someone we'd had our eye on for a while. This is what happened to me - but I am getting ahead of myself.

So, as I was saying, with items in tow I went off to my grandmother's. I always loved the journey there. It took no more than an hour on a good day, and this was a particularly good day. The weather was warm, spring had started early, and the main trail was a carpet of bluebells, so I decided to take my time. After all I was in no rush to get to grandmother's house, so I meandered my way through the sea of blue, picking some of the flowers as I went. I was lost in happy thoughts and blue flowers.

I came to a fork in the road and decided to do a little exploring; after all I was a woman now and could do as I pleased, so instead of going right like I normally would I turned left, which took me deeper into the woods. Everything was lush and green, and the smell of new blooms filled the air. I was completely in my element and entranced; it was so peaceful with not a soul to be seen. Or at least that is what I thought.

As I walked further, I heard the sound of running water, and I decided to follow its direction. Sure enough it led me to a stream, and as I got closer, I heard voices and laughter, but what I then saw still brings me to tears today. A group of boys were pinning another boy down, kicking dirt into his mouth and laughing at their own cruelty. I then saw another boy with a squirming puppy in his hands. He was heading to the water and as he did the boy who was pinned down started to scream louder, but to no avail. I could see what the other boys were planning to do, and I simply could not let it happen, so I yelled as loud as I could. They all stopped, surprised looks on their faces as they saw me. They stared, then one of them yelled the word girlfriend, and something else I couldn't hear, to the screaming boy and they all laughed even louder.

The boy holding the puppy was getting closer to the water and I knew I had to stop him. I grabbed a stone and hurled it at him; it hit him straight in the middle of his face. Now he and the others were no longer laughing. The boy dropped the puppy as he clutched his face, screaming "you whore" at me, then he and another boy rushed at me. I panicked and ran but they were faster, and it didn't take long until they caught up with me.

They grabbed me around the waist and threw me to the floor; one even dared to try to put his hand up my dress! I screamed and kicked as hard as I could, but nothing seemed to work. I closed my eyes wanting whatever was going to happen to just be over with, then I felt the weight of one of the boys fall on me, his breathing soft. I dared to peek; he was unconscious, and a lump was starting to form on his head. I tried to move and look around; the other boy was knocked out and was lying motionless on the floor next to me.

I struggled to push the other boy off so I could stand, when a hand touched me. I flinched, scared that the other boy had woken up, but it wasn't him. The hand reached out to pull me up, and once I was on my feet, I found myself face to face with the owner of the hand and staring into the most beautiful deep green eyes I had ever seen.

"Are you ok?" he asked in a soft voice, but I was too lost in the dark pools of his eyes to answer. "Can you hear me?" There was panic in his tone now, and I nodded as I felt my mouth forming a smile.

The voice sounded relieved. "Ah, good. I was walking by when I saw them chase you. Do you know them?" I shook my head, but still didn't speak. The voice abandoned its questioning. Instead I was picked up by a strong pair of arms and carried back to the stream. The voice said something to someone and then I felt cold water splash my face. I blinked, and the spell was broken.

Alert now, I learned that my rescuer was called Isaac and that the boy I had helped was his kid brother Daniel. They lived together in the woods and this wasn't the first time the village boys had set upon and tormented them. Isaac was used to their taunts and physically tough enough to deal with it, but Daniel was only ten and he was frightened.

Isaac explained that the village boys were cruel to them because they didn't understand them and didn't try to get to know them better. "They have the audacity to call me a wolf, when they're the ones that prey on the weak." he said, with a sarcastic laugh.

Saddened, I started to shiver, and I realised that it was getting late and I was decidedly hungry. Isaac and Daniel walked me to my grandmother's house, where she was standing at the door, waiting. As soon as she saw me, she ran and threw her arms around me. "I was so worried." she screamed as she gave me a relieved squeeze. When she let go, she looked me up and down, and panic flashed across her face.

"What happened?" she asked. Then she saw Isaac and Daniel and turned on them. "WHAT HAPPENED?!" she yelled, as they stepped back in surprise. I reassured her that they were friends who had helped me; her face softened, and she invited them to have tea with us as a thank you.

I could have spent the whole evening with them and was sad when it had to come to an end. Isaac and Daniel thanked my grandmother for the meal and set off back into the woods, Before they disappeared into the dark, I ran after Isaac and thanked him again for his help. Then on impulse I asked him if he would come to the ceremony. He hesitated before saying "I'll try." I smiled as I gave him a kiss on his cheek before I ran back inside, and that night I fell asleep looking at the stars through my bedroom window feeling my heart would burst with joy and optimism.

The two days with my grandmother flew by, and before I knew it the day of the ceremony had arrived. My grandmother helped me put on the white dress, then tied the red ribbon around my neck with the blue pendant dangling from it. I was giddy with nerves, not because of the ceremony but because I was hopefully going to see Isaac again. I hadn't stopped thinking about him since the day he rescued me.

Looking back now the main part of the ceremony was boring; all talk about purity, selection and obedience. The evening was the fun part; there was a bonfire in the centre of the village square, with stalls to the sides serving warm drinks, biscuits and sweets.

When we all arrived from the ceremony, everyone cheered and poured us warm mulled wine. The music played fast and loud and everybody danced, talked and laughed. This was the time we girls had been waiting for; when we could be with whichever young man we felt strongly about. Most of the girls partnered up with someone, but not me; I was eagerly looking around for Isaac. As I searched, I caught sight of some of the bullies I had seen by the river. I felt sick seeing them with the other girls.

And, finally, as my eyes began to ache from staring so intensely, I saw him. My heart leapt - he had actually turned up!!

His long dark hair curled slightly over the collar of the white shirt which showed his strong build. He smiled when he saw me, and butterflies invaded my stomach. He walked towards me, bowed his head and kissed my hand; then led me onto the dance floor. We hadn't spoken yet, but words were unnecessary as his beautiful green eyes locked with mine once more.

I was transported to heaven; nothing else mattered as long as I was with him. I don't know how long we danced for; time became irrelevant. As his movements slowed his heart beat faster, as he pressed my hand against his lips and kissed it before placing it against his chest.

"I couldn't stop thinking of you." he whispered.

"Neither could I." I whispered back.

He tilted my face up to his and whispered again. "My, what beautiful eyes you have. And what lovely red lips."

"All the better to kiss me with." I whispered back, and he smiled, leaned forward and kissed me. Darkness seemed to engulf me; there was no one around us, no sounds. Just me and Isaac, connected by a kiss.

And that's how I want to always remember him. Isaac was my first love, a love that unfortunately wasn't to last. Three days after that night I learned that he had been killed. The talk was that it was a hunting accident, but I knew different. It was definitely hunting related, but he was the one that was being hunted."

AND THAT, *readers, is where she ended her story. We shivered at the brutality of the truth, and now we partly give thanks to the fairy tale version for turning Isaac into a wolf.*

Please make sure to join us again in next month's issue where we'll be delving deep into a feud between sisters, that all started with a pair of scissors and a man's beard.

11

HOROSCOPE

Life is full of surprises and sometimes all it takes is to think out of the box…I would like to dedicate this story to all those who in challenging times can think outside the box.

by Monika Clough

I've been working as a psychic for the past ten years, using mainly a pendulum. I have created charts for Love, Career, Health and Places, each scaling from 10 percent to 100 percent. Over that time I perfected my work so that within a mere fifteen minutes I was able to give at least basic advice to my clients. Feedback to me was good. It seemed that in the end I was always right, although often not what people had wanted to hear. I'll tell you a story about one particular young lady - let's call her Simona.

I MET Simona about 6 months ago. She came to me for advice about her career.

'I've planned everything in my life, and I've worked

hard, but when it comes to getting to the top, there's always a piece missing in everything I do. It's as if I never have any luck. Now I'm twenty-seven and everything seems lost.' she complained.

I glanced down at my notes from our earlier phone conversation. 'What job did you say you do?'

'I'm an actuary; analysing statistics, calculating risks.'

I looked at the chart I'd produced. 'Well this is showing me that you have a talent for languages and anything related to the body. You could be a beautician, sports instructor or anything to do with travel. And perhaps you should consider working on your own. Nothing big, a family-run business. Maybe your husband might help you?'

'But I don't have a husband.' she objected.

I smiled at her. 'You might not have one right now but I can see that you're concentrating on finding one. You're looking for someone who is capable, with a strong personality. The trouble is, there aren't many of them in your surroundings. Frankly, I feel you would be better off living abroad. I can see you marrying a foreigner.'

Her face registered objection again. 'But that can't be true. All I care about is a career. I've never really wanted to get married. And besides, I love this country. Italy is my home.'

I nodded. 'I understand, but I can only tell you what I see. And I see that you don't think that there will ever be a man who will be right for you or give you what you need. But that is because, I'm sorry to say, that so far you've only met the wrong ones. That's why your job seems so much more important to you, but you need to create a balance. You're feeling everything is a mess right now, so how can you attract anything positive? But once you harmonise your life, everything will fall into place.'

I paused and looked her directly in the eye. She waited

expectantly until I spoke again. 'I think you might find somebody - a man - within two months. I can see something related to the date of December 11.'

Our appointment time was up, and I sensed she wasn't convinced or entirely satisfied by what I had told her, but it was all I could tell her.

I heard nothing further, until two weeks ago, when I received a letter.

DEAR MR PARLOTTI.

I had an appointment with you on 28th October last year. Your service wasn't exactly cheap, but I thought "Whatever, as long as it works" - but it didn't. Although I've followed your advice my life is even worse than it was before. The person you suggested would be The One was a total jerk and a disaster. Frankly I think you should be ashamed of yourself.

I would like to end this letter with a thank you note, but there is nothing to thank you for.

Simona Carlucci

I READ the letter twice before deciding I should give some thought as to how best to reply. I was confused; I'd never come across such a response before.

After two sleepless nights I decided to offer this young lady a second consultancy free of charge. I pulled up her phone number from my booking system and called her. Our conversation was short, and I did most of the talking. The silence after I made my offer was broken by her simple 'I accept.' Two days later she walked into my office.

I rose to greet her, extending my hand to her. 'Hello Miss Carlucci, and welcome again.'

She shook my hand and gave me a shy smile. 'I would

like to apologize, Mr Parlotti. I shouldn't have been so mean in my letter, but I was upset when I wrote it.'

I gestured to a chair, inviting her to sit. 'Don't worry about that now. Let's concentrate on what we can do to change it. Tell me what happened, please.'

She folded her arms on her lap, seeming to use the motion to gather her thoughts, then she spoke. 'After I left here, things were pretty much the same until December. Then my work colleague offered me the chance to spend a week with her in the French Alps. In Chamonix. We arrived there on the tenth of December. I'd never been skiing before, so my friend convinced me to book into a ski school. I started the following day, and that's when I met him, exactly as you predicted. On December 11.'

She looked for my reaction, but I didn't speak. It came as no surprise to me that my prediction had been correct, but my only wish now was to hear the rest of her story. I nodded a silent request that she continue. She stared down at her hands as she spoke.

'His name was Pierre and we clicked immediately. He was a ski instructor and lived locally. So when I got back to Turin after the holiday we were only two hours from each other, and we met up in Chamonix once a fortnight. Everything fitted perfectly, like you said. He was a foreigner, self-employed and he worked in the sports industry. I could see that he would be able to help me build a career and a new life. After the winter season finished, he came to see me, maybe once or twice a month. We were great together but I suppose perhaps that was because we didn't see each other that often. He talked about wanting to live with me but when I tried to discuss practical matters, like me relocating to France and finding a job there, he wasn't very helpful. I was the one who always had to come up with the ideas and I started to get fed up.'

As she paused and stared at me, I saw the watery film in her eyes, and she raised a hand to her cheek to brush away a tear drop that had escaped from them. I reached across and patted her other hand. 'I can see how distressing this is, Miss Carlucci, but try to continue.'

As she continued to wipe the stray tears from both her cheeks she spoke again. 'But the worst happened when he admitted cheating on me, and I can still hear his excuse; he just came out with it all in a phone call to me. *I find you attractive but hard to keep up with. You act like you don't need me at all, you're so unpredictable. You always talk about all the men around you; I thought you were the one who was having an affair. Basically, I'm worried that once we decide to live together you will find me boring and I cannot live with this. I can't live with you or without you, it drives me mad.*

And so, I ended it.'

She paused for a moment, glancing up with the shy smile that was now becoming familiar. 'I still see him occasionally, but it's only physical - when I feel I…need that - but it's now nothing more. And the thing is, Mr Parlotti, and what gets me the most, is that everything about us seemed to match so perfectly together. After all this happened, I even saw an astrologist who prepared a chart for me and said that my future husband should be a Sagittarius. And guess what? Pierre's birthday was on November 28. So even the horoscope was correct, yet it still didn't work. So maybe it's me. Maybe I've done something wrong. I really don't know. It's quite frustrating.'

I could see her struggle to understand etched on her features. Something felt wrong here, and I needed to understand what, and to help this girl. I moved to my desk and picked up my pendulum.

'Let me have a look at this. Please, take fifteen minutes

to get some air and come back. I will have some answers for you.'

WHEN SHE RETURNED, she took her seat and gave me an enquiring look. I wasted no time telling her what the pendulum had told me.

'I can see that you made a huge impact on this man's life, but as far as your relationship is concerned, it's giving me only 60%, which is not a lot. You can make it work but it will always be on the edge. Personally, I don't think it has much chance of a future. But there's something else. This Pierre doesn't seem to be the man I was talking about last time we met. There is someone else around you. You have actually already met this person, and in his case the pendulum's showing me 100 percent. Can you think who it might be?'

The stress on her face eased, as if hope had returned, but she looked puzzled. 'No, not at all. But I'll try to think, and let you know, if that's ok? At least I understand that Pierre is not the right man and never was. And again, I do apologize for my letter and for blaming you. You've been so kind helping me today.'

As she stood to leave, I placed a hand on her shoulder. 'No need to apologize, and if you come up with something give me a call. I'm sure we can find an explanation for all this.'

What an extraordinary case, I thought.

Over the next few weeks, new clients and new life stories came and went. I almost forgot this case, until one evening the phone rang. It was Simona.

'Oh, hello, Miss Carlucci. How are things?'

The excitement in her voice radiated down the telephone as she answered. 'You wouldn't believe what happened!'

I smiled into the phone. 'As long as you are not mad at me. And, please, tell me.'

'Since I last saw you, I did a lot of thinking, but didn't discover anything until a few days ago. A member of our staff had been ill - she handles our admin - and we all had to take our turn to cover her work, so we kept on top of it. I dreaded the day it was my turn. I am really rubbish at admin, so I struggled a bit. Then my boss gave me the task of booking a plane ticket to London for our foreign expert, who was returning home. You're probably wondering why I'm telling you all this, and there was nothing special about it, until - when I started to fill in his passport details - I got a shock!

Guess what? He was born on December 11! As soon as I saw the date, I felt like my heart stopped and then the memories came back. Paul, that's his name, joined our company at the end of November. You see, we were getting ready to launch our non-life insurance products and he was helping with all the licensing work. I remembered that he'd invited me to have lunch with him a couple of times, but it was when I returned from France and my head was full of Pierre, so I ignored him really. My colleagues all liked him a lot; he was extremely good looking and fun, but I thought I'd already put my pieces of the puzzle together, so I wasn't interested in looking elsewhere.

What I didn't realise was that although the pieces fitted, they created the wrong picture. So, it turns out you were right, after all. Who would think that the date you saw was important wasn't only the day I met Pierre but also a link to someone's birthday?

Anyway, I accompanied Paul to the airport, and we

talked non-stop. In fact, he nearly missed his flight because we lingered over coffee and didn't want to say goodbye. We've been messaging and talking every day since and I'm flying to London to see him this weekend. I can't wait and …Mr Parlotti? I know he's the one. I've never been so sure of anything.

I just had to tell you and say thank you. You were great.'

She hung up before I had a chance to say anything.

But I looked down at my pendulum on the desk and smiled. What was there to say anyway?

From that day I keep reminding myself that life is full of surprises and sometimes all it takes is to think out of the box.

12

PERSEPHONE: CHAOS-BRINGER

"certe dea carmine digna est" (Ovid 'Metamorphoses')

by Hannah Mortimer

Kore was an immortal and so, by the very definition of her being, could not grow out of childhood, but the cruel beauty was that nor could she enjoy lingering out of time. She was every age and no age simultaneously; an adult and a child, a woman and a nuisance. And irrespective of her own wishes, desires and desperation, she would eternally be Demeter's daughter. Innocent, youthful, beautiful little Kore.

Kore, who was dismissed with a flick of the wrist and an order to go and play in the forest with the young nymphs who she envied being allowed to grow older; to pluck flowers from their roots and weave flower crowns; to arrange beautiful collections of nature and wildlife.

. . .

KORE RIPPED the life from the flowers, crumpling the white lilies in her angered, lily-pale, fist. She flung the flowers into the deep pool of water in front of her, banishing them from her grasp. The pool seemed unendingly deep and she wondered how deep a pool must be to drown an immortal. The only respite to the soul-sucking darkness of the void of water was the glint of ripples on its surface, catching the sunlight and reflecting it back into the calmed sky. Beneath, the water sank eternally down to the very core of the earth, taunting Kore with its release from the earth's tether – as she remained tethered from her ties to her mother.

She threw herself down to the ground, grabbing fistfuls of grass and yanking them from the ground, dirt clinging desperately to the roots of the plants, before she threw them away from herself once more. The mockery of a tantrum haunted her; the spears of the earth landing limp in her youthful hand. She could not bear being infantilised for another moment, being treated as nothing but her mother's daughter. Even nymphs were given more respect than she was, and they weren't even immortals! Jealousy was unbecoming of a goddess, but oh, how sweet it tasted! Oh, to be a nymph, or better still, human. To be mortal.

Kore ripped up another handful of grass, shredding it between her fingers, tossing the corpsed plant to the wind. A few green stalks landed in the ripples of Pergus, tossed about by the faint wind for a few moments, before the water lapped on top of them and they disappeared into its depths. Depths she wished she could disappear into as she urged more white lilies to grow by beheading the flowers, even as they bloomed to maturity, and throwing them on to the black waters of Pergus; watching it slowly turn white with its covering of funeral flowers. Some petals had ripped in Kore's vicious attack, and bled a sweet, sticky nectar over her hands.

'What a violent massacre you've caused, sweet niece.' drawled a voice from behind her. Kore paused her attack and turned to face her uncle. Hades leant against a tree, the shadows of the forest growing darker behind him, shading the clearing in a dark veil, hiding the two of them from any spying nymph eyes.

'There are no souls for you here, Hades.' Kore grumbled, tossing more flowers into the water. She didn't look her uncle in the eye, refusing connection, refusing to submit to the belittling tone he would no doubt start to use. 'Leave me.'

Hades did not speak. He sat silently in the grass with the young deity and listened to her, as she wove her complaints and her daisies together, twisting them into a crown with her deft, nimble fingers. Kore's complaints were not petty, not to her at least, and Hades let them swarm into the air, fluttering through the clearing like gentle bees wandering aimlessly from plant to plant. As she spoke, Kore calmed, gradually settling from agitated pacing to standing, then to sitting, and finally to lying down among the grass and flowers and staring up at the endless stretch of blue sky. Dark hair cascaded on the ground, a halo of black surrounding the Goddess of Springtime and Flowers, coating the ground in an artificial shadow.

Hades leaned back, one hand propping him up from the ground. He plucked the crown woven by Kore, the white petals of its flowers turning golden at his touch and placed it on the forehead of the goddess. It covered her eyes, the rich wildflowers blinding her with their soft gold, reflecting the summer's light. She lifted the crown off her face and raised an eyebrow at the God of the Underworld; scepticism and faux-disapproval preceding uncontrollable giggles. She couldn't refuse the giggles their exit although she hated their childish sound bubbling through the air.

But Hades joined in, his face reflecting the surprise of his own low, rumbling laughter.

The nymphs returned, and Kore turned to Hades with a panic that she hadn't felt before.

'Take me with you.' she pleaded. Her hand clutched at his robes, her white fist shining against the dark cloak he wore. Her grip was tight, unnaturally tight. It was the grip of a girl who would not let go until she got what she wanted, and Kore wanted this badly. This time she was not going to succumb to being the obedient child.

Hades looked down at the lithe figure clutching at him with such desperation, and wordlessly swept her away, an arm around her waist.

The nymphs looked on; horror stricken across their faces. They could do nothing but watch as Hades stole away the prize of Demeter, leaving behind a trail of flowers in his wake.

They were too far away to hear the sheer joy in Kore's laughter, to see the release in her face. They were oblivious to Hades' wry amusement as he whisked away his niece.

IT WAS to grow into a love which defied and defined the passage of time. Kore's revolt from her mother was to cause Winter and Autumn to gain their lives, but she couldn't know that yet. Consequences were for the future; for now, release was all she craved, a freedom to know herself, to build her image how she pleased - to be more than simply Demeter's daughter.

There was no pressure on her to choose which world she wanted - home or the underworld. Hades gestured to the exit as they strolled through the gardens of the dead, reminding her that she was welcome to come and go as she pleased. He allowed her to roam freely, to grow whatever flowers she wished in his meadows and to talk to any of the mortals she envied so much. Kore blossomed with the world she was given. No bounds created, no limits, everything simply spread out before her.

Then the deaths rolled in, human after human, all frail and thin, all speaking of the death of the land. Demeter had scarred it in her anger, robbed it of its nutrition and used the death toll as her bargaining chip.

CHOICE STOPPED BEING a freedom for Kore. She looked on in horror at the chaos her absence had wrought, looked at the lengthening queue of the dead milling on the banks of the Styx. Even the mists of the Underworld couldn't mask the sheer numbers that demanded entry.

A pomegranate sat in her hand, the pomegranate that she had nourished to life. She had brought fruits to the Underworld, and now this one was to decide her fate. If she ate it, her mother would never forgive her, would never forgive Hades. Demeter would take back the harvest, never to return it, and would burn the world in her wake. Kore looked down at the pomegranate.

She picked out six seeds, placed them carefully into her mouth, and chewed. Freedom burst into a flourish of flavours. Her eyes stayed on the fruit until she had swallowed the seeds in their entirety.

She looked up, staring into the soul of Ascalaphus.

'Tell Zeus I'm ready to bargain.'

So spoke Persephone, Chaos-Bringer, Goddess of Spring and Queen of the Underworld.

13

LOVE UNDER LOCKDOWN

To my bestie, my sister from another Mr. - my rock, Laura. Girl, our video chats kept me sane through this lockdown. To Mum, don't worry, I love you just as much as Dad. To my guardian angels; Daddy, Nan & Grandad (R.I.P.)
And, of course, to my mischievous four-legged friend. My fur baby Oscar.
I love you all.

by Nicole Conway

We all know how it started; how life as we knew it ended and we ended up here instead. In lockdown; living 'the new normal'. And let's face it - at first, we all liked the idea of having some unexpected time off work. Time to slow down, recharge and reconnect with ourselves.

But when the summer came and left, the novelty of free time wore off. Fast. No more girls' nights in with cocktails and gossip, no more family Sunday lunches, trips to the cinema, football games in the park. Meeting new people became a thing of fear, helping people was left to the brave. Police patrols roamed the streets and food shortages became more frequent. After the initial collective 'be kind to each other' mantra wore off, the virus brought out the best in some, and the worst in most; fear slowly began to over-rule logic and common decency.

When the days turned to weeks, weeks into months, and when those months turned to years, I lost track of time completely. By the end of the first year I had read every book in my house; most of them twice. I painted so many paintings I had a small art gallery in my spare bedroom. Yet the boredom wasn't the hardest part; it was the solitude. I missed my friends, my family, even Kate the bitchy girl from work. We missed out on birthdays, Christmas, weddings, births - all the moments we took for granted, everything precious.

Thankfully, I had Boxer my beautiful French Bulldog to keep me company. Boxer was a gift from dad when I left home to pursue my dream of being a ballet dancer.

'I never want you to come home to an empty house.' he'd said. Now more than ever I understood what he meant.

Boxer plays a vital part in this story; without him this story would never have happened at all, and I would never have met my Prince Charming.

I was happily doing my daily yoga...*Oh, really? Who am I kidding?* I haven't done a day's yoga in my life; I can barely touch my toes to tie my shoe laces. The truth is I was watching some repeated crap on TV and tucking into a tub of Ben and Jerry's when I heard a crash in the kitchen. Boxer had decided he didn't like the food in his bowl but thought something in the bin smelled good enough to eat. A week's worth of rubbish and old take-out was now decorating the kitchen floor.

'Boxer! For God's sake, move.' I pushed him away from

a chicken leg with a dust pan and brush in my hand, which he looked at with a surprised expression.

I knew why, as I started clearing everything up. I smiled at him. 'OK, so you've probably done me a favour. I've been too lazy lately, and this bin needed emptying a long time ago.'

And that's how this story really started. When I ventured out into the rain to my wheelie bin and Boxer decided he wanted to star in the doggie version of *The Great Escape*. He bolted.

'Boxer!' I yelled after him. I ran from street to street, peering into gardens, calling his name while hiding around corners and trying to be inconspicuous. When I saw the police patrol, I froze. In a moment of fear that I might have lost my only companion in this chaos, I felt the overwhelming weight of the pandemic. Defeated, lost, and all at once totally alone, I stood looking to the heavens - hoping, praying for a ray of light in the darkness. And then I heard it – a deep, melodic, silky-toned voice.

'Is this who you're looking for?' I looked in the voice's direction, and there he was. Standing behind a small brick wall that was covered in white and red rose bushes, and holding my mischievous four-legged friend, stood a man so handsome he could have been mistaken for a movie star.

At least six-foot-four-inches of tanned, muscled maleness with thick blonde hair pulled back into a man bun, he had just enough beard to be sexy that framed a strong jaw; deep brown eyes you could get lost in; and a smile so big and bright I almost forgot it was raining.

'Yes, thank you.' I stammered, brushing the mop of wet hair off my face, painfully aware of the mess I looked.

He lifted one eyebrow and I could sense a smile in the silky voice. 'Odd weather to be walking your dog, don't you think?'

'I wasn't walking him. I went to empty my bin and he bolted. I couldn't catch him.' As I spoke, he opened the gate and Boxer came running to me.

'Thank you for finding him.' I smiled with relief as I picked up my drenched and excited dog. I needed to get us both home and out of this rain. As I turned to head back, I glanced up to thank his rescuer one more time, but he'd gone.

BOXER and I were finally both dry and snuggling up together on the sofa when my phone pinged with a text from an unknown number.

'Hi, its Andrew, the guy from the rain. I hope you and Boxer got home safely?'

I was stunned. How on earth had he got my number? But my heart skipped a beat. Andrew. His name suited him.

I texted back, asking how he'd found my number, and felt instantly stupid when he replied *'It was on his collar. I was about to call when I saw you looking for him.'*

We spent the next two days texting each other. I learned that he had moved to the UK from New York only two weeks before the lock down, so he knew no one here; that he had a younger brother and a twin sister back in the States, and that he loved music, movies and cooking.

I told him about leaving home to be a ballet dancer, but that it hadn't worked out, so I'd wound up in car sales. I told him of my love for art, cooking and anything creative. We talked so much it was as if we had known each other for years.

A week later he finally called me. 'Hey, Roxy, we've been talking now for a week. I guess it's only polite that I ask you out on a date.' My heart skipped another beat as the silky voice continued. 'So, can I cook dinner for you on Friday night? Say around 8 at my place?'

I smiled into my phone. I wished it could happen, but I had no idea how. We'd been on world-wide lockdown for over a year now; how did Andrew plan on pulling this off?

'I'd love to, but how?' I asked. I could hear him returning my smile in his voice as he replied with two words 'You'll see,' before ending the call.

On Friday afternoon I heard a knock on my door. I opened it to find a box on my doorstep overflowing with food, wine, and a large bouquet of pink, red and white roses. I reached down to read the card attached to the flowers.

'Check your emails – I'll see you at 8.'

I ran to my laptop, and there it was. A new email with a link to an online video chat room, and simply signed 'A xxx.'.

I grinned uncontrollably as I unpacked the food, chilled the wine and arranged the flowers in the only vase I possessed. As I admired them and their heady scent filled my small flat, the grin gave way to panic. I hadn't been on a date in what felt like forever, and in our current circumstances I hadn't expected to be going on a date at all.

I turned to Boxer. 'What the hell do I wear? Let's go for a walk and later you can help me decide.'

AFTER EMPTYING the contents of my wardrobe onto my bed I finally settled on the classic "LBD"; my lucky little black dress. I curled my hair and spent way too much time putting on my makeup and picking the right earrings before I almost lost track of time.

I ran into the living room and grabbed my laptop, setting it on top of my kitchen counter. The chat icon popped up on screen and I clicked on it to see Andrew in his kitchen, dressed in a pale blue t-shirt and jeans.

'Wow, you look beautiful.' he said, smiling at me through the screen.

'I feel slightly over dressed.' I half stammered as I felt a blush rising in my cheeks.

He grinned and winked at me. 'No, I'm underdressed, but I always dress down when I cook; I make too much of a mess otherwise. Do you have the box of groceries?'

I glanced in the direction of my fridge. 'I do. What are they for?'

'Well I said I would cook dinner for you, but the only way that works is if you cook with me, so grab the box and follow me.'

We spent the most wonderful hour cooking together as we laughed, joked and learned more about each other. He laughed out loud when I almost burned the pasta and I cried out when he almost cut off his finger cutting onions. When dinner was ready to be served he excused himself, and when he came back on screen he had set the table with a red table cloth, a clear vase with one single red rose and candles that thankfully didn't disrupt the breath-taking image that now sat in front of me.

Andrew had changed into a black tailored suit and a crisp white shirt that was open at the collar to reveal a few tendrils of light brown hair. As we ate dinner over webcam, he put on some music and asked me to dance. Standing back from the camera he swayed from side to side, picking up his tablet and 'virtually spinning me around.' He had thought of everything; it was the perfect first date.

After dinner and dessert, we both settled on our own sofas, cuddling up and watching the same movie on TV as we drank more wine. We stayed like that until we both fell asleep and I honestly don't know who fell asleep first.

I woke up the next morning hearing his voice. 'Morning sleepy head.'

I rubbed my eyes and stretched, trying to remove the kink in my neck from sleeping on the sofa. When I looked at my laptop Andrew was fresh as a daisy in jeans and a red plaid shirt, man bun tight on his head, and freshly shaven as he smiled at me.

'Morning, what time is it?' I asked, catching a glimpse of myself on camera, mascara smudged down one eye, hair like a messed-up birds' nest, quickly trying to make myself look presentable.

'Breakfast time.' he smiled back at me. I looked at my screen and couldn't make out the background; it looked as if he was holding his phone and running. Everything was a blur.

'Andrew, where are you?' I asked.

'Delivering your breakfast.' he grinned.

I ran to the door just in time to see him wave at me from down the street, rounding the corner back to his house. I looked down to find a plastic box on the step with a note attached. It read '*Eggs Benedict, your favourite if I recall.*'

I smiled to myself, and decided he was the perfect man.

For the next year and a half, Andrew and I lived our relationship on screen; only a few streets apart, yet sometimes it felt like he was worlds away.

We could only glimpse at each other briefly in person before he would run away from my door, or me from his after dropping parcels off to each other. We spent our evenings cooking together, watching movies, keeping each other sane. The first time he told me he loved me was at once the best moment of my life but also the hardest, because all I wanted to do was grab him and kiss him and never stop. When his brother got sick, and I watched him cry in fear he was going to lose him, I just wanted to hold him, to be there, and let him know he wasn't going through this alone.

In that moment the full weight of the lockdown came crashing down on me. I'd coped with the boredom, with the days blending into one, with seeing family and friends only through a screen. But seeing how much the man I loved needed me when I was locked behind my own front door, made me realise how powerless I was. Suddenly I could empathise with the princess held captive by the dragon; I desperately wanted to be the valiant knight on the sleek horse riding into battle against the evil witch.

And just as suddenly everything in life made sense.

When the things we take for granted are cruelly taken away from us; the hug of a friend, a handshake, a child's innocent laughter, the loving embrace of a mother and father - then we realise what life is all about. In that moment I saw how easily I had allowed myself to sometimes cherish things over people, and how wrong that had been.

Nothing was more important than human connection. Love for each other is priceless.

Summer came around again. It was a beautiful evening and I was tucked away in my room with a glass of wine and a new book Andrew had left on my doorstep that morning. I was engrossed in the story, blissfully unaware that yet again life was about to change. My phone beeped, chimed and rang all at once as Boxer started to bark with excitement as he ran to the door.

And then I heard it all; the long unfamiliar sounds of people cheering, fireworks, car horns, and laughter. Could this be happening? I ran to the door and opened it to see the streets full of people embracing each other, shaking hands, couples kissing. It was the most beautiful sight I had ever seen. Relief, happiness and pure joy radiated off every person. It wrapped itself around me, pulling me in.

'We are free! It's over!' People cheered. The air was electric with celebration. The lockdown had finally lifted!

All I could think of was Andrew. I grabbed my shoes, gave Boxer a hug and ran out of the door. I kept running as fast as I could, until I was breathless, and the air hurt as it hit my lungs.

I saw the man I loved running towards me, and time stood still.

My heart beat so wildly in my chest I thought it was going to explode. Emotions I didn't even know I had ripped through my veins, racing against the adrenaline. We stopped in front of each other, both gasping for breath, neither of us knowing what to do, or say. For a moment we just stood, then in unison we smiled at each other.

Andrew slowly lifted his hand and brushed a hair from my face, gently tracing my cheek with his finger, the sensation of his first touch running through me like a power surge. His eyes burned with an intensity that made me shake with longing as he broke the silence. 'I've wanted to do this for the past year.'

I wrapped my arms around him and clung to him; I never wanted to let go. Then intensely we kissed. A kiss I never wanted to end.

In a world where we had been forced to be apart for so long, we were finally together.

We had found love under lockdown. And I knew it was a love that would never end.

A Note From Charlotte

Thank you for reading *UNLOCKED*. On behalf of all the storytellers, I hope you have enjoyed the stories, which it has been my pleasure and privilege to curate and edit.

We would all be grateful if you would support us further by taking a few moments to post a review of the book on Amazon, as ratings and reviews are key to any book's success.

AS A PUBLISHED AUTHOR MYSELF, I currently have two books available on Amazon:-

MY NOVEL -*THE CERBERUS AFFAIR* - is an adventure thriller, with a hint of romantic suspense. It is set in the world of cutting-edge genetics research, where a mysterious organisation threatens to derail a ground-breaking discovery that could change human life forever.

LATE NIGHT SHOTS is a collection of short mystery

and suspense stories, designed to entertain and intrigue before lights out.

BUILDING a relationship with my readers is important to me, and I post regularly on my social media pages.

YOU CAN FIND me on Instagram at *charlottevalentinewriter*

and on my Facebook Writer Page at *charlottevalentinewriter.*

THANK you again for supporting *UNLOCKED*.

Acknowledgments

This book would not have been produced and published without the support and help of others, and this is my opportunity to thank them.

I am indebted as always to Anna - my technical guru, marketing adviser and, above all, friend. Much of the credit for the final formatting of *UNLOCKED* for publication, and for designing and producing the cover goes to her - with my gratitude.

I owe thanks also to Alison Apasa who proofread the entire manuscript - a task I hope she will be happy to reprise on my future books!

I also of course want to thank all thirteen authors who are featured in *UNLOCKED* - for accepting my 2020 Lockdown Writing Challenge; for their willingness to work with me on putting this collection together; and, above all, for becoming friends.

Finally, as always, I thank the four-legged people who share my Spanish home, my life and my writing & editing space; my dog and cats. They never cease to show me unconditional love.

Charlotte V.